PENGUIN BOOKS
MAHASHWETA

Sudha Murty was born in 1950 in Shiggaon in north Karnataka. An MTech in computer science, she teaches computer science to postgraduate students. She is also the chairperson of the Infosys Foundation. A prolific writer in English and Kannada, she has written nine novels, four technical books, three travelogues, one collection of short stories and three collections of non-fiction pieces. Her books have been translated into all the major Indian languages and have sold over 150,000 copies.

ALSO BY SUDHA MURTY

Fiction

How I Taught My Grandmother to Read and Other Stories
The Magic Drum and Other Favourite Stories
Dollar Bahu

Non-Fiction

The Old Man and His God

Mahashweta

SUDHA MURTY

PENGUIN BOOKS

PENGUIN BOOKS
Published by the Penguin Group
Penguin Books India Pvt. Ltd, 11 Community Centre, Panchsheel Park,
New Delhi 110 017, India
Penguin Group (USA) Inc., 375 Hudson Street, New York, New York 10014,
USA
Penguin Group (Canada), 90 Eglinton Avenue East, Suite 700, Toronto, Ontario,
M4P 2Y3, Canada (a division of Pearson Penguin Canada Inc.)
Penguin Books Ltd, 80 Strand, London WC2R 0RL, England
Penguin Ireland, 25 St Stephen's Green, Dublin 2, Ireland (a division of Penguin
Books Ltd)
Penguin Group (Australia), 250 Camberwell Road, Camberwell, Victoria 3124,
Australia (a division of Pearson Australia Group Pty Ltd)
Penguin Group (NZ), 67 Apollo Drive, Rosedale, North Shore 0362,
New Zealand (a division of Pearson New Zealand Ltd)
Penguin Group (South Africa) (Pty) Ltd, 24 Sturdee Avenue, Rosebank,
Johannesburg 2196, South Africa

Penguin Books Ltd, Registered Offices: 80 Strand, London WC2R 0RL, England

First published by EastWest Books (Madras) Pvt. Ltd 2005
Published by Penguin Books India 2007

Copyright © Sudha Murty 2005, 2007

All rights reserved

10 9

ISBN-13: 978-0-14310-329-5   ISBN-10: 0-14310-329-6

Typeset in Sabon by S.R. Enterprises, New Delhi
Printed at Gopsons Papers Ltd., Noida

To all those women in our country who suppress their emotions and suffer silently because they have leukoderma. May they be imbued with hope and courage.

_____

There had been an emergency at the hospital that night. A woman with a serious heart condition had gone into labour, and Dr Anand had stayed at her side the whole night. By the time the child was delivered, Anand was exhausted. He gazed at mother and child, wondering whether the precise moment of birth was determined by the baby or its mother. Though he was relieved that the mother had come through the ordeal alive, there was still a nagging worry at the back of his mind. The newborn had not cried at all. Anand and his boss, Dr Desai, shied away from considering the possibility that the infant was dead. Surely, they had not struggled the whole night to deliver a dead baby. . .

As a last resort, Anand tried to resuscitate the girl through artificial respiration. His rough lips had barely touched the delicate mouth of the infant, when she whimpered.

Dr Desai smiled happily, confident now that the baby would survive.

The paediatrician, too, sighed with relief. 'Hey, Anand, isn't she lovely?' Dr Desai and the paediatrician left the operation theatre. The baby was crying lustily now, and Nurse Prabhavathi smiled. Having grown old working in the maternity ward, she was used to such scenes. For a moment, Prabhavathi was lost in thought. Even though the female child is stronger than the male child at birth, as adults it is the man who becomes the oppressor, and the woman who suffers. Why did this happen? She did not know the answer—she only knew that it was a fact of life. Prabhavathi cut short her musings and hastened back to her work as she caught sight of Anand.

Dr Anand was passionate about his vocation. Like most doctors, Anand had discovered that his time was rarely his own. He was soon busy recording the details of the case, but stray thoughts kept drifting through his mind. Both parents play equally significant roles in the birth of a child. But at the moment of birth—the moment of truth—the only reality is the mother. She is the one who sheltered and nurtured the baby within her body while the father watched from the sidelines. Through the window, the sun's rays glinted on his spectacles, and Anand realized that another day had begun. A quick look at the clock showed that it was already seven o'clock. He was no longer on duty and could go home now. He washed his hands and was about to leave when Prabhavathi approached him. 'Sir, Dr Desai left his watch near the operation table. Could you please give it to him on your way home?'

Anand knew how special the watch was to the professor. Dr Desai had done his postgraduation in England as a young man, and had worked under a very famous gynaecologist there. When he had finished the course, his mentor had presented the watch to him, and Dr Desai had treasured it ever since. He often spoke of his teacher and everyone at the hospital knew the story of the watch.

Anand had once teased him in class, 'Sir, to whom will you pass on your watch?'

'Good question! I have no intention of parting with it at all. But I will buy a new watch for the student who scores the highest marks in the final examination.'

Anand glanced at his own watch. It was a gift from his dear teacher and proof of his academic prowess, of his having secured the highest marks in the final examination. Though he was tired, he felt it was his duty to take his professor's watch back to him. Dr Desai was extremely absent-minded, and would probably turn the house upside-down as soon as he realized that his watch was missing.

Anand got into his Mercedes and drove towards the professor's house. Dr Desai stayed in a comfortable bungalow on the college campus. An eminent doctor and teacher, he was totally committed to his work. He would often joke, 'I know the entire city because half of them are my patients and the other half my students!'

When his car entered the professor's bungalow, Vasumathi, Dr Desai's wife, was pleasantly surprised to see Anand; they were distant cousins. The only son of affluent parents, Anand was shy and reserved, and although he was related to the Desais, he had never visited their house without a reason. 'Come in, Anand!' Vasumathi said. 'This is a surprise! What brings you here so early in the morning? I'm sure it must be something very special. In all the seven years you've been in this college, you've come here only thrice. Is everything all right at home?'

'Everything is fine. The professor forgot his watch at the hospital and I thought I'd restore it to him. I knew how upset he would be.'

Knowing her husband, Vasumathi could not help laughing. 'Anand, now that you're here, do have a cup of tea,' she insisted.

'No, akka, avva will be waiting for me at home.'

Hearing Anand's voice, Dr Desai came out of his room, and his face lit up when he saw his watch. 'Anand, don't behave like a baby. You're a young man now. Why must you rush home like a calf running to its mother? When I left for England I was younger than you and had to do everything myself. . .'

'Everyone knows your England story. Once you start, you won't stop for the next half-hour. That may be one of the reasons why Anand never visits us,' Vasumathi interrupted him. 'Anand, you must stay back for lunch today. My brother, Shrinath, has come from the US. He would love to meet you. If you like, I'll call Radhakka and tell her.' Anand felt very uncomfortable. He was so tired that he wanted to go home and sleep immediately. But he was unable to refuse the invitation. Noticing his silence, Dr Desai said understandingly, 'Anand, I know you've had a hard night. You can go and rest in the guest-room upstairs until lunch is ready.' Vasumathi nodded in agreement and, feeling helpless, Anand went upstairs without a word.

The guest-room was clean and neat, but had none of the trappings of wealth that filled his own house. Anand had his nightclothes with him in his carry-bag. He changed quickly and lay down on the bed so utterly exhausted that nothing seemed to matter—not food or clothing or company. He just wanted to sleep. But the moment his head touched the pillow, he heard a sweet voice say, 'Darling, you are handsome and irresistible. . .you are the very picture of Manmatha. When I saw you today, through the branches of the parijata tree, I fell in love with you immediately.'

Anand was dumbstruck. For a minute, he thought that his imagination was playing tricks on him. He could make out from the voice that the person who had spoken was a young woman; and he was so startled by what she had said that he was wide awake now. He looked around carefully, but there was nobody there.

Anand was tall and fair, and had curly hair and a charming smile. His cousin Anasuya, his junior in college, often came home and told them the stories about Anand that were being circulated in the ladies' room of the college. Girls would follow him just to talk to him, and Dr Desai himself had often said, 'I wish I had a daughter. I would have made you my son-in-law.' He had every quality that a young girl could desire in a man. He was not only handsome, but well-bred and intelligent too.

Anand smiled at himself in the mirror. Who could have seen him there and fallen in love with him at first sight?

Outside, the birds were chirping. The fragrance of the parijata flowers wafted in through the windows. Anand sat on the bed and waited for the voice to resume speaking. But there was absolute silence. He felt ashamed of his presumptuousness—how could he have imagined that someone he had never seen had fallen in love with him? He was about to lie down when he heard the same clear, sweet voice once again, 'I feel I have been waiting for you for many lifetimes. You are my ideal man.'

Now Anand was sure that he was not imagining things—somebody *was* talking to him. The words were coming from the other side of the wall. The woman was apparently explaining how she had fallen in love with Anand to a friend. But he could not hear the other person's reply. He felt more than a little awkward about what he had overheard, but perhaps that was the way girls usually spoke to each other. . .he was not sure. His sister, Girija, was always so aggressive and wrapped up in her own world that they were hardly close. Anand rarely had even a casual conversation with her.

He got off the bed and stood with his ear to the wall so that he could hear even the softest whisper from the other side. He assumed that a couple of girls were discussing him.

'Love is not a commodity that you can buy after putting it to the test. It is not something that you can buy after consulting others. It is not sold in the market for money. When you see a man and your pulse starts racing, your blood begins to sing and you yearn to spend the rest of your life only with him, sharing his joys and sorrows— that is love. It is irrepressible; it cannot be crushed under any circumstances. Who he is, or what his family is, or where he works is immaterial to me. I love him whole-heartedly. I do not know whether he loves me or not. He may not even be aware that there is someone who loves him so much. But my love for him is as firm as the Himalayas and as clear as the waters of Manasarovar.'

This declaration of love—notwithstanding the sweet voice and the sweeter words—was so theatrical that Anand was astonished. In a voice filled with sadness, the girl appealed humbly, 'Like Rohini to Chandra, like Lakshmi to Narayana, am I to him. Just as the creeper depends on a tree, I depend on him. I cannot live without him, and for his sake, I am ready to renounce everything. Let society say anything it wishes. I do not care. . .'

In between the conversation he could hear the clinking of bangles. As far as he knew, Dr Desai had two sons. Shrinath was married and his wife was a doctor in the US. From the sound of the voice that he had just heard, he guessed that the girl was not more than twenty. And there were no young girls in Dr Desai's house. Hoping to hear more, Anand waited a little longer. But there was complete silence.

Anand stepped away from the wall and went towards the adjacent room, hoping to see the lovestruck girl. The

Sudha Murty

door was closed but not latched. With great hesitation, he pushed it open. But to his surprise there was nobody there. There was not even a trace of anyone having been there a few minutes ago!

Disappointed, Anand went back to his room. His sleep had vanished completely. So he sat on the bed and tried to recall what had happened. Was it a hallucination, or a dream?

He was unable to figure out the answer. But he wanted to meet the girl who had fallen in love with him at first sight, from behind the parijata tree. He wondered if she was as sweet as her voice.

∽

It was evening and the professor was deep in conversation with his friend. Normally, no senior doctor went to the hospital in the evening, but Dr Desai was particular about making the evening rounds, talking to patients, and spending some time with his visitors. And when senior doctors like him were so conscientious, juniors like Anand could not miss the evening rounds.

Anand was in the professor's waiting room, preparing some notes for the next day's class. Dr Desai had told him firmly, 'Anand, I am meeting my friend after a long time. If there are any visitors, tell them I am not here and deal with them yourself.'

As Anand sat at his desk, he kept remembering what had happened in Dr Desai's house the previous week. He was still perplexed by the incident. He had expected to see the girl whose voice he had heard at lunch but the only other person present had been Vasumathi's brother, Shrinath. He had not told Vasumathi about what had happened. Vasumathi and Dr Desai had a droll sense of humour, and it was quite likely Vasumathi would embroider the whole story and even tell his mother, Radhakka, about it. 'A female spirit in our house is haunting Anand. Perhaps she is the enchantress Mohini! Is this Mohini from the college campus or did he meet her somewhere else? Get him married as quickly as possible!' she would say.

Anand shivered at the mere thought of putting himself in such an embarrassing situation, and felt it would be best to remain silent about what had happened that day. His reverie was interrupted by a sweet voice.

'Excuse me, can I meet Dr Desai?'

Anand looked up from his notes, and was stunned to see a young girl of extraordinary beauty standing before him. He had met countless girls over the years, but never had he seen anyone so startlingly lovely. With her beautiful large eyes, exquisite complexion, and face framed by long, jet-black hair, she looked like an apsara. She was wearing a green cotton sari with a blue border and a blue blouse. When she smiled at Anand, deep dimples appeared in her cheeks. The expression on her face suggested that she was accustomed to such a reaction, and she repeated her question. 'Can I see Dr Desai?'

'I'm sorry, Dr Desai is not here,' Anand said, remembering his surroundings.

'But that's not true. I know he's here.'

'I'm sorry, you cannot see him now. Why don't you tell me what you need?' Anand wanted her to stay for some more time.

For a moment, she frowned. Then, her brow cleared and she said, 'Will you kindly tell him that Anupama has come?'

Sudha Murty

What an apt name, thought Anand. She was truly 'incomparable'.

'In that case, will you wait here? I'll go and tell him that there's a patient waiting for him.'

Anupama smiled like a parijata flower blossoming at the touch of a dewdrop. 'Excuse me, I am not his patient, Mr—?'

'I am Dr Anand.'

'Oh, I see. . .!'

She never got a chance to finish her sentence as Dr Desai and another gentleman came out then. He looked at Anupama and exclaimed, 'Anu, how long must I wait for you? Here you are chatting pleasantly with Anand, while an old man sits inside waiting for you! I was about to leave now.'

'Uncle, selling tickets is not an easy job. I had to coax and cajole people to buy them, and I've been here for a while. . .' For a moment, Anupama was in a quandary. What was she supposed to say. . .that Anand had prevented her from going in? She quickly collected herself and said, 'Let it be. Now, which ticket should I give you?'

'Oh Anu, I forgot to introduce my friend, Dr Rao. He is the principal of the Arts College. You may know him. And this is Dr Anand, one of our most brilliant doctors, who is shortly going to England for further studies. He is one of the lucky ones blessed by both Saraswati and Lakshmi.'

'Sir, please. . .' Anand mumbled, embarrassed.

Dr Desai ignored him and continued. 'Anand, this is Anupama. Her father, Shama Rao, and I have been good friends since school. What can I tell you about Anupama; she is so talented. . .'

Anupama tried to stop Dr Desai. 'Uncle please, don't talk about me. Just buy the tickets. That is more than enough for me.'

But the doctor would not be stopped. 'Anand, you cannot imagine how versatile our Anu is. She is a superb actress and an excellent student, always getting the top rank. She even sings Hindustani classical music. Which gharana do you belong to, Anu?'

'Uncle, enough of my praises! Please buy a thousand-rupee ticket.'

Dr Desai smiled, 'Anu, I am a poor man with no private practice. I cannot afford your thousand-rupee demand. Give me two tickets of a hundred each, instead. The principal is also like me. Give him two tickets of a hundred each as well. Is that all right, Dr Rao?'

'Of course, Dr Desai. That is my budget, too! I won't be in town on the day of the show, but my daughter will definitely be there. She wouldn't want to miss your play,' the principal responded.

Anupama looked crestfallen, the thousand-rupee tickets still in her hand. Looking at her, Desai continued, 'Anu, don't worry. You can still sell your thousand-rupee tickets. Our Anand can afford to buy them all.'

Anand wondered why he should buy the tickets without even knowing what the tickets were for. Hesitantly, he said, 'Please give me a hundred-rupee ticket, too.'

Anupama had already torn off two thousand-rupee tickets from her book. She wrote Anand's name on them and said, 'Doctor, two thousand is not a lot of money for you. But for an institution that helps physically challenged children it is a big sum. They will be grateful for your donation. This is a fund-raising programme. Please do not

Sudha Murty

refuse to buy the tickets. Please come with your wife to our play.'

Anupama talked like an experienced saleswoman, and when she held out the tickets, Anand felt too shy to refuse her.

'Hey Anu, Anand is not married yet. Though there is a big line of hopeful women in front of his house. He wants to marry someone of his choice; and who that is, nobody knows. On his behalf I will guarantee that he will come,' Dr Desai concluded.

❧

Anand woke up later than usual the next morning. Although he had not been on night duty, he had been unable to sleep the entire night. Thoughts of Anupama had occupied his mind all the time. Dr Desai had used many superlatives to describe her and although Anand did not know anything about her other qualities, he had certainly felt the impact of her beauty. He was sure she would outshine any beauty queen.

But beauty and histrionic talent were two different things, so her play might not be so great, he told himself. He was debating whether to go for the show. But his heart told him he had to see her again; he had to get to know her. After all he had met her only once, he knew nothing about her. Not even whether she was married or single, although from what he had seen there was no indication that she was married. But what did she think of him? His musings were cut short when the razor blade nicked his cheek and blood started oozing from the cut. He imagined Anupama standing behind him, smiling. He felt elated and light-hearted at the very thought of her. Whistling happily, he got ready to go for the play.

The Town Hall was crowded and Anand realized that Anupama must have worked really hard to sell so many tickets. While looking for his seat somewhere close to the front row, he met Vasumathi. 'I knew you would come,' she said, smiling mischievously. 'Anu gave me complimentary passes for the boys but there are no seat numbers on them. And they're pestering me for ice cream. Let them sit in your seat while I get the ice cream. Could you go and find Anupama and ask her the seat numbers of my complimentary passes?'

'Where is she?'

'She is in the green-room behind the screen. But you can ask anybody, they will direct you to her.' Without even waiting for his reply, Vasumathi went away.

Happy, but somewhat hesitant, Anand went looking for Anupama. He found her sitting in a chair, simultaneously giving instructions to several people. Clad in a deep red sari, she reminded him of a beautiful rose. Her long hair was loose and touched the ground like a dark cloud. She was holding a garland in one hand and a book in the other. Anand felt as though he had entered the court of a queen, and not a green-room! Though he went in and stood near her, Anupama was so busy that she did not even notice him until a girl standing nearby whispered to her. A faint blush stole across her cheeks, as she asked, 'Where are you sitting?'

'Oh, I have found my seat. But Vasuakka's complimentary pass. . .'

Anupama had no time to hear him out. She was in a hurry. 'Oh, they can sit on one of the red sofas and you may also sit with them if you want.' And then someone called her and she went away. As she brushed past him,

Anand felt as though a beautiful parijata tree had showered its flowers on him.

There was no reason for Anand to keep standing there, but still he did not move. Anupama did not come back though she had said that she would return in a few minutes. Then he remembered that Vasumathi would be waiting for him, and would make many suggestive comments if he delayed going back to the auditorium. So, he reluctantly returned to his seat. Anupama returned to the green-room moments after Anand left.

Her friend, Sumithra, whispered in Anupama's ear, 'Anu, who is this Prince Charming? Is he one of your admirers?'

'Come on Sumi, don't imagine too many things. I sold him tickets worth two thousand. Is it not my duty to help him? It is purely professional! Anyway, I have to go and wear my make-up. You handle things now.' Anupama dashed off.

❧

It was a fund-raising programme—so there were several speeches about social responsibility, humanity, and so on. Anand was slightly bored; he knew that when people got hold of a mike, they hated to part with it. Every minute seemed to last a year.

Finally, all the speeches were over, and a melodious voice off-stage began to speak on the play that was to follow: '*Kadambari* is one of the earliest novels written by the great scholar Bana Bhatta, in Sanskrit. A part of this novel has been translated and dramatized by Ms Anupama. The essence of the novel is the love between the heroine,

Mahashweta, and the hero, Pundarika. The cast includes Ms Anupama as Mahashweta, Ms Nirmala as Pundarika. . .

'Mahashweta is an extremely beautiful princess and the daughter of the king of Gandhara. One day she goes on a picnic with her friend, Kadambari, and meets Pundarika, the dazzlingly handsome son of a rishi. It is love at first sight for both of them. . .'

As the princess, Anupama looked sculpted in ivory. When she enacted a love scene with Pundarika, her face glowed with passion. She delivered her lines so naturally: 'Darling, you are handsome and irresistible. . .you are the very picture of Manmatha. When I saw you today, through the branches of the parijata tree, I fell in love with you immediately.

'I feel I have been waiting for you for many lifetimes. You are my ideal man.' Anand realized instantly that these were the exact words he had heard in Vasumathi's house that afternoon. In his ignorance he had presumed that the unseen girl had been talking about him. As he heard those words again, he thought, *Thank God, I did not discuss this with anybody. Anupama must have left by the rear staircase the other day, which was why I did not see her.*

The play continued. Later, Mahashweta confided in her friend, 'Like Rohini to Chandra, like Lakshmi to Narayana, am I to him. Just as the creeper depends on a tree, emotionally I depend on him. I cannot live without him, and for his sake, I am ready to renounce everything. Let society say anything it wishes. I do not care. . .'

Pundarika, Mahashweta's beloved, meets with an untimely death and the princess, wearing a white sari and garland, undertakes a severe penance in the forest. Her resolve is unshakable. Her dear friend, Kadambari, tries her best to dissuade her, but to no avail. Finally,

Mahashweta's heart-rending love for Pundarika brings him back to life and the lovers are reunited.

Anand looked around—Anupama's portrayal of Mahashweta was so convincing that the entire audience was spellbound. Anand realized that Dr Desai had not exaggerated. Truly, Anupama was not only beautiful but also a brilliant actress.

When the play ended, there was tremendous applause as the president of the association called Anupama to the stage and spoke highly of her commitment to their cause. 'Ms Anupama has been of immense help in raising funds for the school. I thank her on behalf of the organization. She has not only been involved with the play but has also sold a substantial number of tickets. We would like to present her with a memento in appreciation of her efforts.'

Anupama had not expected to be singled out for such praise and was taken aback, but humbly accepted the gift. Lost in admiration, Anand sat still, raptly following her every move.

⤐

As Anupama collected her things and prepared to go home, Vasumathi approached her and said, 'Anu, the play was wonderful! It is quite late, how will you girls get back to the hostel?'

There were three other girls with Anupama.

'We'll take an auto or a taxi,' Anupama replied.

'It's too late to take a taxi. Anand's house is nearby. I'll tell him to drop you off on his way home.'

'No aunty, we'll manage.'

But Anand was only too happy to help, 'I'll drop all of you back,' he said.

They were all tired and one of the girls whispered in Anupama's ear, 'Let's get a lift.'

Anand opened the back door and all four of them squeezed in. Anand had hoped that Anupama would sit in front with him. Foolish thought! A girl like Anupama would certainly never do anything so forward. She was only aggressive when it came to selling tickets!

Anand drove in silence and the girls, too, did not talk. When they reached the hostel, all of them alighted, and Anupama said, 'Thank you, doctor.'

'You're welcome, Anupama. Your play was excellent.'

'All thanks to people like you who bought tickets and encouraged us to host the show.'

Anand smiled and started the car. He was leaving behind him the most beautiful girl in the world. . .and his heart.

All the girls turned towards their respective rooms, too tired to talk. Sumithra and Anupama, who shared a room, continued to walk together.

They had been friends and room-mates for the last six years. They were like sisters, and could sense what was going on in each other's mind. Although they were poles apart in nature, they liked each other a lot, and their lives had become intertwined. Whenever she bought a new sari, Sumi would insist that Anupama try it on first.

While changing into their nightclothes, Sumi asked suddenly, 'Anu, where did you discover Dr Anand?'

'Sumi, don't be silly! It seems he is Desai Uncle's assistant. Quite a rich man, too. . .Somehow I managed to sell him two thousand-rupee tickets.'

'When did you see him first?'

'A fortnight back. When I was in Desai Uncle's house. I was rehearsing for the play, and saw him from the first floor. He had come in his Mercedes. I'd hoped he would

Sudha Murty

buy the thousand-rupee ticket. But I left as soon as you called and told me to return to the hostel, so I could not meet him that day. Later, I went to the hospital to sell tickets and met him there.'

'Anu, you are a super saleswoman! By the way, you were fabulous as Mahashweta today. When you were sobbing for Pundarika, I felt like coming onto the stage and wiping away your tears.'

Anupama laughed.

'Tell me more about Anand.'

Anupama was about to lie down on the bed, but at that she sat up and said dramatically, 'Miss Sumithra Devi, I do not know anything about this Anand, who is the alter ego of Pundarika, and with whom it seems you have fallen in love. If you command me, I will dig up all the details and get back to you at the earliest. I will also convey your feelings to him. Now, it is past midnight and I would like to sleep. Please, may I?'

Sumithra was annoyed. 'Anu, you play so many roles in college dramas that acting has become second nature to you. You can hide your true feelings from everybody but me. Today you did not act. I know that you have lost your heart to Anand—he is *your* Pundarika. That is why you played the role of Mahashweta so realistically. Anand's eyes never strayed from you. I know you will not be able to sleep tonight,' she concluded triumphantly.

Anupama remained silent. She turned her face towards the wall and, through force of habit, started reciting her lines: 'Like Rohini to Chandra, like Lakshmi to Narayana, am I to him. Just as the creeper depends on a tree, emotionally I depend on him. I cannot live without him, and for his sake, I am ready to renounce everything. Let society say anything it wishes. I do not care. . .'

'Princess Mahashweta, this is not your palace. This is the girls' hostel. And, fortunately, your Pundarika is not in the forest. He resides just a stone's throw away. Please go to sleep. . .and goodnight!' Sumithra laughed.

Sudha Murty

Though Anupama would not admit it, Sumithra was right. Anupama had felt herself drawn to Anand ever since she saw him from the first floor of Dr Desai's house. Vasumathi had spoken of Anand occasionally, and he had captured her heart the moment she set eyes on him. As Mahashweta, when she had talked of love at first sight, she had been speaking from her own heart. However, she was a practical girl, well aware of her situation. Given the difference in their backgrounds, she knew that it would be unrealistic on her part to dream of a life with Anand. She was the eldest daughter of a poor village schoolteacher, and destined to struggle all her life. She was aware that Anand was favoured by Lakshmi, the goddess of wealth. Though she herself had the blessings of Saraswathi, the goddess of learning, Anupama's life had never been an easy one. She also had no clue as to what Anand felt about her, and did not wish to end up with a broken heart. Reaching out for a star in the sky would only lead to disappointment.

This was the first time she had kept a secret from Sumi. Anupama had always shared her thoughts and feelings with her. But, somehow, she was reluctant to breathe a word about her feelings for Anand.

Anupama woke up early the next morning to prepare her notes. Sumithra, who was still lying in bed, mumbled lazily, 'Anu, the play was just yesterday. But you're up so early as usual. You always work so hard. Don't you need a break?'

'Sumi, if I don't work hard I will lose my scholarship and that will be the end of my career.'

Sumithra sat up hugging a pillow and said, 'Anu, you are completing your post-graduation this year. Why are you worried now?'

'Sumi, that is the very reason I'm worried. You know that from the first year of college till now, I have survived on scholarships. If I don't secure a good rank, I won't be able to do my PhD and I'd have to find a job.'

Sumithra was silent.

It was true that Shamanna could not afford to pay for his daughter's education. His wife Sabakka, Anupama's stepmother, had told her husband categorically, 'Let us not educate her further. It might become difficult to find a husband for her. Besides, she will not support us. She has to marry and go to somebody else's house one day.'

Anupama had been devastated. But, fortunately, she had won a scholarship and escaped from her stepmother's clutches. Sabakka and her daughters, Vasudha and Nanda, did not like Anupama. The main reason was that Anupama was very good-looking and her stepsisters were plain. Sheer jealousy prompted them to taunt Anupama by saying that just because she could write a few lines she was too proud of herself.

Shamanna was a timid man. He was completely subservient to his second wife's will, and was not in a position to help his eldest daughter as it was ultimately Sabakka who made all the major decisions at home. But fate had been kind to Anupama. An endowment by a generous donor for educating a girl child from the village, stipulating that if she performed well she would get a stipend every year as long as she wished to study, had come to her rescue. Anupama, who was in the final year of her MA, was still eligible for this scholarship.

In four months, Sumithra and Anupama would go their separate ways. Sumithra would go back home and get married. Though her family was very well off and could afford to pay enough dowry, sadly her dark complexion would still pose a problem.

Sumithra would often tease Anupama, 'Anu, when I stand next to you, I could ward off the evil eye from you.' To which Anupama would say, 'Sumi, don't talk such rubbish!'

Over the next few days, Anupama exercised enormous self-control and banished 'Pundarika' from her mind, concentrating on her studies instead.

&

Anupama was never far from Anand's thoughts. He did not know anything about her save that she was a gifted actress and a lovely girl. Anand had occasionally day-dreamed about the woman he would marry one day, and he was certain of one thing—she would be beautiful. The shadowy figure that had been hovering on the edges of his dreams now stood unveiled. Anupama.

His mother was a domineering woman. She was always nagging Anand to get married. But he had not given it a serious thought so far. Anand wanted a beautiful bride; his mother wanted one who could match their status in the community. Finding a girl who satisfied these conditions was proving to be rather difficult.

But now, Anand could see his bride clearly. It was Anupama, with her fair complexion, beautiful long hair and dimpled cheeks. But he did not know what she felt about him, or to which community she belonged, or even whether she was already engaged to somebody.

Deep in thought, he came to the terrace outside his room. The lovely parijata blooms reminded him of Anupama. He tried to recall the first time he had heard about her. It had been in Dr Desai's house. Surely Vasumathi's brother, Shrinath, would know about her. Feeling elated, he went to call Shrinath.

'Shrinath, I want to talk to you about something.'

'Oh! No problem. . .you can come to akka's house.'

'Not there. Let us meet somewhere else.'

Shrinath agreed to wait for Anand at the Kamat Hotel. Anand had never been in such a situation before, and he began to grow more and more nervous—waiting for the university results had been less nerve-racking.

Shrinath looked at him shrewdly and said, 'What, doctor, you look like a patient today!

'Oh, it is nothing. Why didn't you come to see the play?'

'I watched some of the rehearsals when Anupama and her friends came to akka's house.'

'Is that so?'

'Yes. After all, her father is my brother-in-law's friend.'

'Where is she from?'

'Oh, so that's the reason you have invited me here for tea,' Shrinath said shrewdly. 'If I had known this earlier, I wouldn't have settled for anything less than a dinner!'

'Yes, I do want to learn more about Anupama,' confessed Anand.

'Why? Do you want to marry her?'

'Yes.'

'Do you have the courage to disobey your mother and marry her?'

Once again despair clouded his mind. Did she belong to some other community, or was she already engaged? A

Sudha Murty

beautiful girl like Anupama might have been 'spoken for' a long time back.

Shrinath read his mind. 'Anand, she belongs to our community, but she is from an extremely poor background.'

Anand was relieved. He knew that his mother was very keen on money, but as long as the girl belonged to the right community, she would come round. Shrinath, however, was more worldly-wise. He tried to point out that Radhakka might not be happy with a match that was not of the same status, but Anand said joyfully, 'Avva will agree. My happiness is more important to her than money.' His filial love had made him blind to his mother' weaknesses.

Shrinath kept quiet.

≈

When Anand told Radhakka that he had chosen the girl he wished to marry, she listened in silence. Radhakka was a woman of few words. She never let her emotions get the better of her. No one could ever make out what was going through her mind. Though Radhakka was in her early fifties now, traces of her beauty still remained. After all, she had not known much suffering in her life. Radhakka had sharp, piercing eyes that never held any sign of gentleness or friendliness. On the contrary, her striking looks made people nervous. They sometimes said that if she had been born in the last century, she would definitely have been a queen.

Her late husband, Gopala Rao, had been a very successful contractor, but he had always been scared of his wife. They had two children, Anand and Girija.

Anand was born five years into her marriage—the result of many pilgrimages and prayers for a male child. He was the apple of her eye, a fountain of joy in her barren life.

She would smile when he smiled; and when he wept, gloom would descend on her. Even though they had several servants at home, it was she who fed and looked after him. Anand grew up in a sheltered environment. He was good at studies and extremely obedient to his mother. He always felt she was the person responsible for all his progress. Anand inherited his mother's looks and his father's intelligence.

His sister Girija was born five years after him. She had been brought up like a princess. Good-looking and extremely arrogant, Girija behaved harshly with everybody, and nobody had the courage to remonstrate with her. Radhakka would always find excuses for her conduct, 'Oh, she is only a child, after all,' she would say. Girija was not good at studies, but no one bothered about it.

Their house was named Lakshmi Nivas. It was aptly named in every way—it was a big mansion in a large plot of land. Every Deepavali, Radhakka would organize a big puja for the goddess Lakshmi, and the entire town would be invited for the celebration.

Radhakka was extremely orthodox and narrow-minded. When her husband died, the thought that she was a widow made her feel very uncomfortable although she had no financial worries. With the death of her husband, she felt she could no longer celebrate the puja of the goddess, given the attitudes and conventions prevailing in the small town where she lived. She believed that only Anand's wife could now perform the Lakshmi puja, and she was waiting for him to get married. Although he had won a scholarship to go to England for higher studies, Radhakka would not let him go until after his marriage.

<small>❧</small>

Sudha Murty

The village schoolmaster, Shama Rao—Shamanna, as he was called—was teaching mathematics in the verandah of his home to a group of students who were all from well-off families. In keeping with the usual custom in the village, no money was paid to the teacher, but the children brought him coconuts, vegetables or other produce from their fields.

Shamanna's mind was not on what he was teaching. He was impatiently waiting to hear the sound of the village postman's cycle bell. Since the small village was located some distance from the district headquarters, the postman came once a week. He not only delivered the letters, but, if necessary, also read them out and wrote the replies as dictated to him. He would stay at the village master's house and leave the following morning for the next village.

Vasudha, Shamanna and Sabakka's daughter, was helping her mother in the kitchen. Though Sabakka was busy chopping vegetables, she came out every five minutes to see if the postman had come.

The postman, Papanna, brought a pile of letters when he arrived. There were two letters for Shamanna. He opened one and began reading. The children noticed that he was occupied and started whispering among themselves, the whispers quickly turning into a quarrel. The noise distracted Shamanna. He was already upset by the contents of the letter, and this unruly behaviour angered him further.

'Children, go home now. For your homework, write out the multiplication tables from twenty-one to thirty, three times each, and show it to me tomorrow.'

The children behaved as if the doors of a cage had been opened, and they disappeared within moments.

The letter Shamanna was reading was from the father of a boy who had come with a marriage proposal. Anupama, though the eldest, had told her father very clearly that she did not want to marry just yet as she wished to pursue her studies, or start working. She had also requested her father to go ahead with Nanda's marriage. As Nanda was not interested in studying and was ready to get married, he had tried to arrange her marriage, and she had been 'seen' by a prospective bridegroom and his family.

It seems your eldest daughter Anupama is doing her MA in the city. Our son happened to see her in a play and liked her immensely. If you do not object to it, instead of your second daughter, we would prefer an alliance with your eldest daughter. We do not expect any dowry. Whatever you choose to give will be sufficient. We will be very happy if you accept this proposal. Please do not misunderstand us. After all, marriages are made in heaven. We are sure Nanda will get a better match.

'Oh, is there a letter from the Patils? It's been a while since they came to see Nanda,' Sabakka asked excitedly when she came from the kitchen.

'Yes, the letter is from them. But they have not approved of the match.'

The colour drained from Sabakka's face. 'That day they spoke as if they wished to go ahead with the alliance. What made them change their mind?'

'Well, they have changed their mind now.'

'Why?'

'The same old story. This boy, too, wants to marry Anupama,' Shamanna replied hesitantly, knowing what her reaction would be.

Sabakka was furious. 'When did that fellow see Anu? We never even mentioned her name! Did you say anything?'

'No. It seems he saw her in a play.'

Sabakka's anger knew no bounds, 'This apsara won't get married herself and insists on destroying my girls' lives!'

The sound of Nanda's sobbing fuelled Sabbaka's animosity towards Anupama. She went in and tried to console her heartbroken child.

Shamanna started reading the next letter. When he had read it, he was overcome with surprise. He re-read it to make sure he had understood the contents correctly. He could hardly contain his joy and excitement as he called out to Sabakka.

'What is it? I am busy.'

'Do you remember my old school friend, Dr Desai?'

'Ah! That famous professor. . .Will you tell him to find a good bridegroom for our daughter?' Sabakka was desperate to see her own daughters married. She said, 'I have two daughters to be married, and looking out for suitable alliances is no joke. You need not worry about Anu. She will always have boys chasing after her.'

'Stop talking rubbish about Anu. She would never look twice at any boy. If the boys chase after her, it is not her fault. Dr Desai has written about a boy. His name is Anand. He is also a doctor. His father was Gopala Rao, a very famous contractor.'

'We will never be able to match their expectations. Tell the doctor to suggest someone within our reach.'

'That is true. But, Anand has seen Anupama and. . .'

'And what?' Sabakka's heart skipped a beat. She fervently prayed that such a rich boy would not choose Anupama.

But God was deaf to her prayers.

'Dr Desai has written that Anand likes Anupama and has asked me to send Anupama's horoscope to Anand's mother.'

Sabakka was silent.

'What do you think?'

'Anything I say will appear unkind. I am only her stepmother, after all. You are her father, so you decide.'

Shamanna tried to reason with his wife. 'You are her mother. Anu has always been respectful towards you. Why do you always find fault with her? If the boy likes her, it is not her doing. Tell me what you think.'

'If you really want to know my opinion. . .don't proceed with this match. There is no comparison between their financial status and ours. Marriage should always be among equals. What is wrong with my brother, Ranga? He might be a little dark but he has a diploma in engineering. So what if the age difference is ten years? He won't ask for a paisa. Talk to Anupama, she will listen to you.'

'No. He is not the right match for our Anu. As a mother, you should not suggest anything like that.'

'I do not differentiate between Anu and Nanda. If Ranga agrees to marry Nanda, I will be all for it.'

Inside, Nanda was gazing at the ceiling of the old house. There were cobwebs everywhere, and the sun was peeping in through the broken tiles. She told herself, *Even if everyone agrees to this, I will not.* . .She knew very well that Ranga would never approve of her dark skin and large nose.

Shamanna did not talk until lunchtime. Sabakka took his silence as a positive sign. 'Please think it over. Let us not proceed. We neither know who these people are, nor what their intentions could be. Isn't it a little unusual that such a rich and handsome doctor wants to marry our poor daughter? There might be something wrong with the boy that they have not disclosed.'

'I want to send Anu's horoscope to them. Desai would not have written to me without verifying all that. He knows we are not rich. This is a godsend to us. I will not be able

Sudha Murty

to find a better match than this for Anu even if I spend my life searching for it. If Anu says no, I will convince her to agree; she is still young and does not know what the world is like.'

Shamanna got busy copying Anu's horoscope. Sabakka lit the lamp in front of the family deity and prayed that the horoscopes should not match. Nanda, on the other hand, silently wished that the horoscopes would be compatible, so that Anu would finally be out of her life.

Unaware of the tornado brewing at home, Anupama continued with her studies.

✦

Radhakka was silently swaying back and forth on the swing in her home, Lakshmi Nivas. Her confidant and advisor, the family priest, Narayana, sat before her as if awaiting her orders.

'Avva, what will you do now?' Radhakka was 'avva' to everyone.

'Narayana, do the horoscopes really match? How is the girl's horoscope?'

'Avva, the horoscopes match perfectly. The girl's horoscope is excellent.'

'Anand is my only son. What about children?'

'Oh, her horoscope shows only male children.'

Of all the horoscopes that had been matched with Anand's, so far this horoscope was the most compatible.

Girija walked in while they were talking. She was in her first year MA and had seen Anupama in the college. Radhakka asked for her daughter's opinion.

'Avva, she is poor but very good-looking. No wonder Anand likes her,' she said.

Radhakka was lost in thought. She could not think of any plausible arguments against this proposal. On what basis could she refuse her consent to this match? Anupama's poverty was the only drawback. But she could not cite that as the reason for her objection; people would call her greedy. She wondered what stand she should take. If someone as pretty as Girija admitted that she was good-looking, which boy would not want Anupama? If Radhakka rejected the proposal, Anand would probably argue with her about it. What if he insisted on marrying the girl regardless of what she said? She would lose face, and that was the last thing she wanted. Then another thought struck her. What if Anand went to England without getting married and brought home an Englishwoman as his wife? The very idea made Radhakka break out in a sweat. The community gossips would say, 'Look at Radhakka's son, he's brought home a foreigner for his wife. Serves Radhakka right for being so choosy.' How could a woman from another land uphold the customs and traditions that had been handed down to them by their ancestors and had now become inextricably woven into the fabric of their lives? She thought of the family, the children, the inheritance, the grandchildren, and she shivered. Surely, it would be better to have a poor girl as her daugher-in-law rather than a girl from another community. She could not bear to think of the disgrace if that were to happen.

Silently, Radhakka pushed the swing back and forth. She would have to make a crucial decision soon.

If she agreed to the alliance, Anand would be happy. And it would earn her Anupama's undying gratitude. People would praise her, 'Look at Radhakka. . .how large-hearted she is! She has accepted a poor girl when she could have got a daughter-in-law from a better background.'

Gently, she pressed her foot down on the floor and stopped the swing. Her mind was made up now. 'Narayana, choose an auspicious day for the engagement and tell the girl's father that I would like to see her once before that,' Radhakka said wearily.

So, Anupama is going to become my sister-in-law, thought Girija when she heard her mother's decision.

A nupama was surprised when Shamanna turned up at the hostel unexpectedly. He did visit her once or twice a year, but only when he had some official work in the city, and he always informed her of his plans beforehand. He had never dropped in on her unannounced in the six years that she had been away from home. Anupama thought Shamanna looked more haggard than the last time she had seen him. Perhaps the worry of taking care of three daughters on his meagre income made him appear pale and careworn all the time.

'Anu, I want to talk to you about something important. Let's go out for a while.'

Anupama took him to a stone bench under a big banyan tree within the hostel campus. On full moon nights, the hostel girls usually sat on the benches around the tree, and Anupama had often entertained her friends by singing songs late into the night.

Father and daughter sat down and Shamanna explained why he had come. Anupama was surprised. 'Appa, I cannot get married now. I am still in my final year. I want to take up a job and help you financially.'

'Anu, don't be foolish. You won't get a better match than this. You have never been a burden to me. You have always studied on scholarships, and you've been sending me all the money you save. For my sake, please don't say no to this proposal.'

'Appa, these people are very rich. We cannot meet their expectations. If you take a loan, who will repay it? Nanda and Vasudha are yet to be married and there are still two more months to go before I complete my MA' Anupama was taken aback by this sudden turn of events.

'Anu, I have told them about my financial status. Don't worry about Nanda and Vasu. I will get them married on my pension and I promise you that I will not take any loans. You can complete your MA after marriage. By the way, Anu, have you seen the boy? How is he?'

Anupama did not reply. How could she describe Anand to her father? Could she say, *I am Rohini and he is Chandra, I am Lakshmi and he my Narayana. He is irresistible, the very picture of Manmatha, and I fell in love with him the moment I saw him . . .?*

&

It was the day Anand was to meet Anupama, in the presence of the elders in the family, to complete the formality of 'bride-seeing'. Even though the match was certain, Radhakka had insisted on first 'seeing' Anupama before agreeing to the engagement.

Since Radhakka was very traditional, she felt that Anupama should not enter Lakshmi Nivas until after the marriage, and decided to 'see' Anupama in Dr Desai's house. After all, Lakshmi comes in the form of a daughter-in-law and she must enter the house at an auspicious time, with her right foot overturning the measure of rice that would be kept on the threshold, in order to bring prosperity to her in-laws.

Anupama had acted in many plays, but this was real life, and she was overcome with shyness. Pundarika was going to be her husband and her future would be linked with his life. Not in her wildest dreams had she thought that she would meet Anand in such circumstances. Anupama entered the room where Anand sat with his family, Dr Desai, Vasumathi and Shamanna. Since she had nothing appropriate to wear for such an occasion, Sumithra had lent her a brick-red sari. Her long plait, dark red bangles and small drop earrings made Anupama look all the more stunning. Anand's eyes never wavered from her face as she sat opposite him. *Was this the same Anupama who had sold him tickets and acted in the play?* wondered Anand.

Girija looked at Anupama enviously. She would now be a competitor for Anand's affections. All along, Anand had been theirs. Now he would belong to Anupama and there was nothing they could do to prevent this.

Radhakka had taken one look at Shama Rao's threadbare coat and dhoti and immediately assessed his financial position. Noting the absence of the girl's stepmother, she had shrewdly guessed the nature of the relationship between Anupama and Sabakka.

Looking at Radhakka's ornaments, and Anand's Mercedes—symbols of a world totally alien to him—Shamanna had grown so painfully aware of his limitations that he had not spoken at all.

It was Dr Desai who broke the silence, 'Anand, do your want to say anything?' he asked.

Anand shook his head. After all, what could he say? This was hardly the time or place to express his love for Anupama or extol her beauty.

'Anu, do you want to say anything?' asked Vasumathi.

What was there to say? Anand had long heard the song in her heart. . .noticed the glow in her face. Anupama sat without speaking, her head bowed, her eyes downcast.

It was Radhakka who had the last word. 'We have a very large circle of friends and relations, so we want the wedding to be held at our house and at our expense.' Radhakka had carefully masked her disappointment. She was a practical woman and had realized that it would be impossible for Anupama's father to conduct the marriage in a manner befitting their status. This was the only solution—after all, she had to maintain her standing in the community. Radhakka looked at Shamanna and continued, 'You can call as many people as you want. Don't bother about the expense.'

Anand and Shamanna were surprised by her magnanimity.

For the first time that evening, Anupama lifted her head and looked at her future mother-in-law with gratitude. There was no sign of happiness or warmth on Radhakka's face, but there was a knowing gleam in her eyes. For a moment, Anupama shivered.

The wedding was a grand event. Anupama felt as though she was in the midst of a fairy tale. From Anupama's side of the family just twenty people attended the function. She had lost her mother when she was a year old, and so she had not had much contact with her maternal relatives; only her uncle attended the ceremony. As a child, Shamanna's mother had taken care of Anupama, but she too had died within a few years. Sabakka had disliked her stepdaughter from the very beginning. The grand scale on which the marriage was being celebrated depressed her further. Anupama's stepsisters, too, were taken aback by such opulence. Shamanna, on the other hand, could hardly contain his happiness and gratitude. He thought that the goddess herself had come down to earth in the guise of Radhakka.

Almost all of Anupama's friends from the hostel were present at the wedding, as she was very popular with them. Sumithra was constantly by her side, and the day before the wedding, she had asked her mischievously, 'Mahashweta, do you want to talk to your Pundarika? If you have any message, your companion will go and deliver it.' And both of them had burst out laughing .

Anupama's father had bought her an artificial silk sari, for that was all he could afford. Radhakka had been very particular about the way her future daughter-in-law decked herself. She had showered her with many expensive saris and ornaments. While Anupama was trying on a diamond necklace, she overheard Vasumathi whisper, 'Oh, this is only ten per cent of Radhakka's jewels.' This had suitably impressed all the women present.

But Anupama said to herself, *To me the greatest jewel is my Anand. The rest only weigh me down.*

Though Anand wanted to talk to Anupama, he was unable to do so because of the crowd around them. When they were finally alone, he found that she still remained silent. 'Anu, why aren't you talking to me? The day you came to sell tickets, you were talking so freely.'

Overcome by shyness, Anupama did not lift her head.

'Anu, I am giving you my heart today, please keep it safe.'

Anupama smiled and dimples appeared on her cheeks.

❦

A week had passed since the wedding and all the relatives had left. Anupama and Anand had a room in the first floor of Lakshmi Nivas. Anupama had taken a leisurely bath and stood in the balcony, drying her long hair, enjoying the privacy and solitude. Her life seemed a perennial fountain of joy, of

Sudha Murty

love and happiness. She was unable to understand how philosophers could describe such pleasures as temporary.

Anybody would envy her. God had been kind to her and she had married into such a distinguished family without having to face any obstacles. Her only worry was that, within two months, Anand was supposed to go to England for further studies.

Radhakka, too, was upset about the proposed trip and argued incessantly with Anand, 'You have studied so much in our country. Why do you have to go to another country to study further? By the grace of God, we have enough money and you don't have to go there to earn more. Now that you are married, you should settle down here.'

'Avva, I am not going for the sake of money. I am going there to learn new things and it is just for two years. Please don't stop me.'

Anupama could not bring herself to argue with him. She was still adjusting to her new environment and that was making her diffident. Anand told her, 'Anu, this is our only opportunity to go out and see the world. Once we come back we'll stay in Lakshmi Nivas forever.'

Over the next two months, Anand and Anupama went everywhere together; and every minute spent in each other's company was infinitely precious.

Radhakka had eventually reconciled herself to Anand's departure, but she had one wish. Deepavali was only two months away, and she wanted her new daughter-in-law to perform the Lakshmi puja, and then leave for England.

This was not an unreasonable demand and as it was only a matter of two months, Anand and Anu happily agreed to it. It was decided that Anupama would join Anand immediately after Deepavali.

As the day of Anand's departure drew near, Anupama became subdued. Her husband was going to an unknown country, and people had been making malicious comments that she could not ignore. 'One can have a wife here and another there as well. The women there are very aggressive,' they had said.

Anupama constantly feared that something untoward would happen if Anand went abroad. Anand read her mind and said, 'Anu, don't worry. I'll count every hour, every minute and every second till you arrive.'

'Suppose something happens to make you forget?'

'What a foolish girl you are! Haven't you heard what they say in a church wedding? "Till death do us part. . ." And that is my promise to you. We shall always be together. Anu, how can I ever think of anybody other than you?'

Anupama sighed with relief.

❧

Anupama stood gazing at the sky until she lost sight of the aeroplane. She felt miserable and her heart was heavy. Anand had been a stranger to her three months back and now he had become the most important part of her life. She had still not understood fully how that had happened. She looked up at the sky again.

Radhakka understood her confusion and reassured her, 'Don't worry, time will fly very fast. Shall we go now? It will be late by the time we reach home.'

Radhakka, Girija and Anupama had gone to the airport to see Anand off. No one spoke on the drive back home. As they drove through the market, Radhakka remembered that she had to collect some ornaments she had ordered from the jeweller's shop. Radhakka was reluctant to take her new daughter-in-law to the jeweller with her. She did not want her to be dazzled by all the wealth on display and desire more than what was due to her. So she said, 'You buy some vegetables here. I will be back with Girija in a few minutes.'

Anupama did not ask where they were going as she did not want them to think she was prying. She told the vendor to weigh out the vegetables and was standing near the shop, lost in thought, when the driver asked her, 'Madam, avva has forgotten to give me the money. Will you pay for the vegetables?'

Anupama went back to the car to get her purse. She had already taken out the money when she realized that the purse was not hers. It was Girija's. Anand had bought two identical purses when they had gone to Ooty on their honeymoon—one for Anupama and one for Girija. Anupama was disconcerted at the thought that she had handled someone else's purse without asking. As Anupama replaced the money, she noticed that Girija's purse was like that of any other college student. It contained a mirror, a small comb, a packet of bindis, a handkerchief and some money. What caught Anupama's attention was a packet of oral contraceptives hidden inside with a note that said, 'After 10 p.m.'.

Anupama had been taking the same tablets since her wedding because Anand had not wanted children so soon. Finding the tablets in Girija's purse had momentarily stunned her. When the driver returned to take the money, Anupama gave it to him. Confused, she sat in the car thinking about the note. Who was the person Girija was going to meet? Was Radhakka aware of this?

By the time mother and daughter returned, Anupama had managed to calm herself. Girija looked so innocent that, for a minute, she felt she had misjudged her. Worried by the strange look on Anupama's face, Girija asked her at once, 'Anupama, have you seen my purse?'

'No, I don't know where it is.' That was one of the few lies Anupama uttered in her life.

'Girija, you should be careful with your belongings. Otherwise Lakshmi will never stay with you,' Radhakka admonished.

Anupama began to observe Girija's activities from that day on. She dared not discuss her suspicions with anyone. She was too intimidated by her mother-in-law to feel at ease with her. At times, she thought of telling Anand everything. But she had known him for barely two months and did not feel comfortable writing to him on such a sensitive issue; nor did she wish to talk about it over the phone.

੭

It is said that wealth normally never comes alone. It is generally followed by arrogance, and so it was with Girija. She did not pay any attention to Anupama or try to be friendly with her. She had her own room and her own set of friends, and she was always busy with her own activities.

One day, during dinner, Girija told her mother, 'Avva, all my friends have decided to go on a two-day study tour to Belur and Halebeedu. I want to go, too.'

'Will there be any boys joining this tour?' asked Radhakka.

'No, only the girls from our class and our lady teachers are going,' Girija assured her quickly and was given permission to go on the trip.

While Girija was away Radhakka's friend, Sundaramma, who was celebrating her grandson's first birthday, invited her to attend the function. Radhakka had not been feeling well, so she called Anupama and said, 'Anupama, you must attend the function. Give the child a silver bowl as a gift.

Remember to wear your emerald ornaments and take the car. But don't stay too long in their house.'

Radhakka believed that the purpose of attending a function was not so much to socialize or participate in the festivities as to flaunt one's wealth. Her actions were never the result of love or affection. Anupama could not go out without taking the car and the driver, and never without her mother-in-law's permission. Before her marriage, she had been a free bird and had gone wherever she pleased. Now, she felt as if she was locked up in a gilded cage.

She dressed to please her mother-in-law, and left for the ceremony. By the time she arrived at Sundaramma's house, the other guests had departed, and only the members of the family were around. Anupama began talking to Sundaramma's daughter, Kamala, who was Girija's classmate. Casually Anupama asked Kamala, 'Hey, why didn't you go to Halebeedu?'

'What are you talking about?' Kamala looked puzzled.

'I thought the college had taken the girls from your class on a study tour.'

'The college hasn't organized any such trip for us. Now that we're in the middle of our seminars, no one can go anywhere.'

Anupama was nonplussed. She realized that something was wrong, but did not want to divulge any family secrets to an outsider.

Kamala, however, persisted, 'Who told you about the trip?'

'I can't remember. I guess I was confused and got everything mixed up.'

'Where is Girija?'

Anupama stammered, 'Oh, she is not well, so she stayed at home.'

'Is that why she didn't come to college yesterday?'

'Yes!' Anupama was now desperate to escape from Kamala's clutches. 'Oh, it is getting late; I must go now,' she mumbled.

'What's the hurry? Anyway, Anand is not here. Stay for some more time. It seems the school for the physically handicapped is organizing a fund-raising programme this year, too!'

'Is that so?' Anupama had lost contact with the world outside Lakshmi Nivas since her marriage.

'Aren't you acting in their play?'

'Which play?'

'*Chand Bibi*. Now that you're at home, I thought you'd go for the rehearsals. I'm surprised you don't even know about this.'

Sundaramma, who had overheard their conversation, exclaimed, 'It's out of the question. Radhakka will never allow her daughter-in-law to act. Imagine girls from decent families going on stage! Things cannot go on as they did before the marriage. Radhakka will have a heart attack if her daughter-in-law carries on like that!'

Anupama left with a sinking heart. So that was their opinion of such a beautiful art! It meant that, henceforth, she could never act or sing. Her only purpose was to be adorned and exhibited as an acquisition, a reflection of their status in society. She had never expected to live this kind of a life.

Her only ray of hope was that an educated person like Anand would not hold such views. After all, had he not been charmed by her play?

She was confident that he would never let her down.

&

Sudha Murty

When Anupama reached home, she found that Girija had returned from her tour. She was describing to her mother the beauty of the Belur and Halebeedu temples. Anupama behaved as though nothing had happened, and did not breathe a word of what she had heard to anyone.

As the days went by, Anupama began to get bored and depressed. She did not feel at home in her in-laws' house, and suspected that she would always feel like a stranger there. The only comfort she derived was from Anand's calls and letters. They were as welcome as rain during the hot summer, as refreshing as an oasis in the desert. In his letters, he described the beautiful places that he had seen, and also his loneliness and how he yearned to see her. *If only I had wings, I'd fly away to him,* thought Anupama.

One day, Anupama was in her room, reading Anand's last letter over and over again, when Girija walked into the room in a towering rage.

'Anupama, who told you to gossip about me?'

Taken aback, Anupama asked, 'What did I do?'

'It seems you checked with Kamala about the tour.'

'No. I never asked her anything. We were just having a casual conversation. You're mistaken if you think I was trying to pry.'

'No. I'm not mistaken. You had doubts about me, so you asked Kamala.'

'I really do not know whether you went on the tour or not. Only you know about that. But Girija, as your sister-in-law and as someone older than you, can I tell you something?'

Girija did not answer.

'You have not chosen the right path, and your behaviour does not befit the family you come from. That's all I want to say.'

'Oh, stop preaching. Only avva has the right to advise me. Who are you to tell me anything? You have enacted so many love scenes on the stage. Was that all right?'

'They were only plays, Girija. Not real life. You can ask anyone about me—you will not hear a single word of scandal.'

'Just because you have married my brother, do not think you can tell me what to do. You should know your limitations.' Girija was about to leave the room when Radhakka entered. When she saw her mother, Girija's attitude underwent a complete change.

'Avva, Anupama thinks that I did not go to Halebeedu and she asked Kamala about it. I learnt this from Kamala in college today,' Girija began to sob.

Radhakka was furious with Anupama. This girl who had come into their house a couple of months ago was making her daughter cry!

Radhakka raised her voice, 'Is that true, Anupama?'

Things were going out of control. It was as if there was an ocean of misunderstanding between them. Anupama understood the reason for that and said haltingly, 'I only mentioned the trip in passing. . .it was a casual question. I'm sorry if I have hurt you all.' Tears rolled down her cheeks—the first since her marriage. She had hardly ever wept before. Silently, she withdrew to the window, and Radhakka followed Girija downstairs.

'Girija, tell me the truth now. Where did you go?'

'Avva, I swear on goddess Lakshmi that I went on the college tour.'

'Then why was Kamala not aware of it?'

'Kamala belongs to a different batch and we don't interact much with each other.'

Sudha Murty

Since Radhakka did not know that there were no batches at the MA level, she directed her anger at Anupama. 'No wonder they say you should check out the family background before you bring a girl into your home. She wanted to ruin your reputation! How dare she! I agreed to this alliance only because Anand was so adamant.'

Throughout the night, Anupama lay awake; she just could not sleep. Girija's altercation with her had made Anupama withdraw from the rest of the household. She was desperate to go away to England; each day had become a trial for her.

Anupama was not sent to her mother's house for the Gowri festival. Not that Sabakka had been keen on inviting her. Her father had sent her a hundred rupees—a large sum for him—by money order. Radhakka was disgusted. 'The baksheesh I give our cook is more than this,' she muttered.

At last, it was the auspicious day of the Lakshmi puja. All of them forgot their differences as it was the celebration of the year. Every nook and cranny, every room in the house was cleaned till it gleamed. Hundreds of invitations had been sent out and Anupama was decked in silk, gold and diamonds. She was waiting for her visa, and was due to leave for England in a couple of months.

Before the puja, Narayana kept hustling everybody, 'One should not miss the auspicious time; otherwise, Lakshmi won't stop here.'

Radhakka sent Anupama to get the hot coals to light the incense for the goddess. On her way back from the kitchen, a red-hot piece of coal fell on Anupama's foot, severely burning it. She quietly poured some cold water on her foot and went to the hall to continue with the puja.

In spite of the pain, Anupama mingled with everyone; she was the perfect hostess. Radhakka was very pleased that the function was a success.

After the function was over and the guests had departed, Anupama poured some more cold water on her foot. The cold gave her some relief from the pain, but the burning sensation did not subside. By the time she went to sleep, she noticed that the burn had bubbled into a large blister.

Her discomfort persisted over the next two days, but she did not tell anyone about it. She preferred to suffer in silence as she knew that no one there was concerned about her. She applied some medication and though the wound started healing, it itched occasionally.

A couple of days later, she noticed something very odd. There was a small white patch on her foot where she had got burnt.

Sudha Murty

Initially, Anupama did not bother much about the patch. But as the days passed, she realized that it was growing bigger. She could no longer afford to ignore it. *What was it?* she wondered. She began to suspect that it could be leukoderma, and became numb with fear. She was too shocked even to cry.

Radhakka noticed that her daughter-in-law was becoming listless, day by day, and assumed that it was because she was missing Anand. Anupama did not share her problem with anybody.

In the meantime, Anupama's father wrote to tell her that Nanda was getting married. The groom was a clerk in Lakshmi Co-operative Bank, and as his grandmother had passed away recently, they wanted the wedding to be held only after six months.

Shamanna's letter asked if she would stay back for six more months and then join her husband. Anupama was very happy for Nanda, but she was in no mood to postpone her journey by another six months. She wanted to escape from her in-laws' place as soon as possible. Meanwhile, she decided to go for a check-up and if her suspicions about the patch proved to be true, she would also find out how it could be treated.

Anupama had seen many people with leukoderma, but had hardly given them a fleeting thought. However, things were different now. She asked God what sin she had committed to be punished so. As far as she could remember she had never hurt anybody. Then why had this curse befallen her? She prayed to God to prove her fears false. Anupama knew she had to be extremely discreet, and keep her problem a secret. But how could she visit the doctor without anyone else finding out about it? Whenever she wished to go out, the driver had been instructed to take her out in the car. And if she went to the doctor, the driver would definitely report it to her mother-in-law. Nor could she consult their family physician—that would invite an even greater disaster.

Anupama could not share her agony even with Anand. She brooded constantly and prayed to God to save her from this ordeal. But the patch continued to grow, making her terrified of what the future held in store for her.

One evening, when Girija was not at home and Radhakka was getting ready to attend a religious discourse, Anupama decided that it was the opportune time for her to visit the doctor. She said, 'I would like to visit my friend in the hostel. I haven't met her in a long time. I will see her and return soon.'

Radhakka asked, 'How will you go? I will be taking the car and the driver.'

'Don't worry. I can take a bus or an auto.'

'Don't go by bus. Take an auto and come back before it gets dark.'

Anupama felt as if she had freed herself from a giant web. She immediately took an auto and soon reached the clinic of a famous dermatologist, Dr Rao, in the heart of the city. Fortunately, the doctor was in, and Anupama sat waiting for her turn with the other patients who had come before her.

The clock ticked away mercilessly, and Anupama started to worry that she would not be able to reach home on time. She was beginning to wonder why the doctor was taking so long, when she was called in. The doctor was confident and sympathetic, and his reassuring voice stilled her fears. 'Sit down. Don't worry. Tell me, what is the problem?'

Anupama hesitated for a moment, then raised her sari so that her foot was exposed, and showed him the white patch. Dr Rao tested it with a needle and ascertained that there was no loss of sensation there.

His face was expressionless as he said, 'You have vitiligo.'

'What does that mean, doctor?' asked Anupama, thinking it could be some minor problem.

'It is also known as leukoderma.'

Anupama could not stem the flow of her tears any longer.

The doctor was aware that tiny white patches like that had ruined many marriages, shattered many hearts, broken many engagements. Most patients who learnt that they had leukoderma were overwhelmed by the social implications of their affliction. He did not try to stop her from crying—he felt it was the best way for her to cope with her tensions and fears.

When she regained her composure, he said, 'This is not an incurable condition. There are new medicines available in the market today. Before I write out the prescription, can I know a little bit of your family history? Does anybody in your family have vitiligo?'

'My mother passed away when I was a child, so there is none whom I can ask. But I can't think of anyone in the family who has had this. Doctor, is it hereditary?'

'Not necessarily. Nothing had been proved as yet. '

'Doctor, did this happen because my foot got burnt?'

'No. That was just a coincidence. These patches may come anywhere, at any age. There is no explanation for them at all. Some women even get them during pregnancy.'

Anupama wiped her tears. 'Doctor, why did I get this?' she asked.

'I don't have an answer to your question—in fact, no one can answer it. I will write out a prescription for you. Try it and see if it helps you.'

'Do you think I'll be cured within a month?'

'Let me be frank with you,' Dr Rao said. ' Skin conditions do not get cured within a matter of days—the time frame varies from person to person. We will try to arrest it and see if we can stop it from spreading further. But I cannot assure you that you will be cured within a certain time.'

Anupama's heart sank as she rose to leave.

Understanding her agony, the doctor continued, 'Don't lose courage. This is not a disease. It is caused by defective pigmentation of the skin. Face it boldly—anxiety and tensions may only aggravate it.'

'Doctor, will you please keep my visit confidential?' Anupama requested the doctor in a low tone.

'Of course, it is my duty.' He wrote the prescription and gave it to her saying, 'This medicine is a solution. Apply it only on the affected area. Infrared rays are strongest in the morning. Expose this medicated patch to the sun's rays for ten minutes. Repeat this procedure every alternate day, and then come back to me.'

The consultation had taken almost an hour. She now understood why dermatologists spent such a long time with each patient.

Anupama's emotional condition worsened as the days passed, and she was utterly despondent. She was afraid to inform Anand about her condition, and worried about the

Sudha Murty

consequences if she did not get cured. She followed the doctor's instructions very carefully, but it was of no use.

The doctor had tried to reassure her, and told her to be patient. Anupama wondered. . .even if she had endless patience would it solve her problems? What about the people around her? Every time she had to visit the doctor, she had to weave a big lie so that nobody would guess where she was going. . Anupama now felt as though there was a sharp sword hanging over her head. She was haunted by the fear that someone would find out her secret; and the harder she tried to conceal her problem, the larger the web of deceit grew. And so did the patch.

She started wearing her sari much lower than before in order to hide the patch, and as a result at times even walking became difficult. Was she suffering now because of her karma, because of something she had done in her previous birth? Was her affliction the result of someone's curse? She was no longer keen to call up Anand or write letters to him. Her wretchedness made her oblivious to everything else. She felt as though she was walking through a dark tunnel that had no end in sight.

One evening, a few days later, Anupama conjured up a suitable lie and left to meet the doctor. Girija was away and Radhakka had gone to visit one of her friends, but when she reached her house she discovered that her friend was out of town. Radhakka decided to get some saffron from the bazaar on her way home, to add to the milk she drank before going to bed. While she was waiting in the car for the driver to fetch the saffron, Radhakka's eyes accidentally fell on the board outside Dr. Rao's clinic. Radhakka was under the impresion that those who visited dermatologists had venereal diseases. The very thought of those patients was distasteful to her. She was about to look away when she saw Anupama come out of the clinic.

Radhakka was shocked. She could not believe that her daughter-in-law was visiting such a place, and that too, without her knowledge! She had always thought of her daughter-in-law as a simple and submissive girl. Anupama had never crossed her in any way, by word or deed, making this breach of confidence unbelievable.

When the driver returned from his errand, she asked him to take her home immediately. Radhakka's furiously pondered over what she should do next as she made her way back. She had an uncompromising nature and it did not take her long to arrive at a hard decision.

Anupama reached home sometime later, completely unaware of what awaited her there. She walked up straight to her room and found a letter from Anand. He had written about British theatre—the constant innovations and the new plays that were being staged in different parts of the country, Globe Theatre in London and Shakespeare's birthplace, Stratford-upon-Avon.

Anupama, I am really busy coping with the workload at the hospital, but whenever I see anything beautiful, hear a sweet song, or smell a lovely flower, my mind flies back to you. I am counting the days to your arrival.

'Anupama!' Radhakka called out from downstairs.

Anupama was so immersed in reading Anand's letter that she did not hear her.

Anu, life is so beautiful and interesting. I am sure you will enjoy every minute of it. By the way, how is avva? She may be harsh at times, but please don't misunderstand her. For my sake, you should overlook all that. . .

'Anupama!' Radhakka's voice was sharper this time, and Anupama started as it cut into her thoughts. She suddenly realized that something was wrong.

'Yes, I'm coming,' she called out as she reached the stairs.

Radhakka was standing at the foot of the stairs. 'Is your friend's house in the market?'

Anupama fumbled for an answer.

'Come down!' commanded Radhakka.

Anupama only remembered putting her foot down on the step below. Her foot either got entangled in the folds of her sari, or sheer fear blinded her—she lost her balance and screamed as she rolled down the stairs.

Her scream brought the driver, the cook, Narayana and Girija rushing to her. Anupama was unconscious, and blood trickled from the cut on her forehead. Her sari was in disarray, and what she had been struggling to hide so desperately was now revealed to everyone.

All of them stood staring at the white patch on her foot. Radhakka did not say anything. She looked as if a calamity had befallen them, and Girija felt a kind of vicious satisfaction. She thought to herself, *You wanted to expose me, but now you are exposed.*

Narayana said, 'Oh, this is a bad omen!'

Nobody bothered about Anupama. Only the cook brought some water and sprinkled it on her face. She was not badly hurt and recovered soon. Covering up the patch with the end of her sari, she leant against the wall and tried to sit up as Radhakka started questioning her again.

'Anupama, I saw you in the bazaar today.'

'Yes. I had gone to see the doctor,' she replied in a low voice.

'Then why did you lie to me? I thought you had gone to visit your friend.'

Anupama did not reply.

'Since when have you had this white patch?'

'From just a few days back.'

'Oh! Are you sure it wasn't there before the marriage? Don't lie to me. Anand is far too naïve and you took advantage of him. You deceived him into marrying you for his money. '

Anupama protested, 'No, that is not true. I did not have this before marriage.'

Radhakka now directed her anger towards Narayana. 'Narayana, tell me. Did the horoscopes really match well?'

'Certainly, avva. The horoscope that was *given* matched well. . .'

Radhakka murmured, 'Who knows, it might have been someone else's!'

Anupama did not even try to defend herself. Radhakka's verbal onslaught had left her shaken to the core.

Anupama was too sensitive to brush aside what had happened. She was unable to eat that night, and nobody called her for dinner anyway.

Narayana kept telling Radhakka, 'This is a bad disease. She cannot perform any puja now. It must be the result of a sin from her previous life.'

Anupama spent the night agonizing over her future. The next morning, Anupama went to the garden as usual and gathered flowers in the silver basket. Soon after the wedding, at Narayana's suggestion, Radhakka had decided to offer one lakh flowers to the goddess Lakshmi. And Anupama had been assigned the job of collecting the parijata flowers every day.

When she went to the puja room with the flowers Narayana said, 'Don't come in here and pollute everything.' He took the flowers she had collected, threw them outside, and poured some water on the basket to purify it.

Anupama was dumbstruck. She had anticipated some problems because of her affliction, but she had not expected to be ostracized in this manner. Till that day, Narayana had always been humble and subservient, and had spoken to her respectfully because he knew she would inherit Radhakka's mantle one day.

Nobody bothered even to talk to her anymore. Earlier she had taken her meals with her mother-in-law and Girija. But now, food was sent to her room, implying that she was not welcome downstairs.

In the afternoon, Sundarakka arrived and Anupama could hear her talking to Radhakka. Normally, she would have gone down to meet her, but she knew that she would not be welcome now.

'Radha, I heard the bad news through your cook. It is simply appalling! I felt so miserable I had to come and see you even though it is late afternoon. I feel terrible knowing that you have been deceived.' Sundarakka spoke as though she had come to offer condolences to someone who had been bereaved.

'I do not know what to do. How will I tell Anand? Poor boy! He was deceived by her beauty.'

'Radha, be careful. Do you know whether it is leukoderma or leprosy? It might be contagious,' added Sundarakka.

Anupama was stunned. Dr Rao had explained to her that although the clinical symptoms of leukoderma and leprosy might be similar, they were very different in nature. He had mentioned that, with the medicines currently available, even leprosy was curable. But who could argue with the likes of Sundarakka?

A feeling of misery engulfed Anupama. She realized that her position had become lower than that of a servant in just one day. The servant could go home and sleep after finishing the day's work. But where could she go? To her father's house?

That was impossible. She had never felt comfortable in Lakshmi Nivas, but it had been her home until the day before. Not any longer! A home, after all, is not made up of just the four walls—there must be affection and love, as well.

So where was the place she could call home? Where would she find kindness and trust? With Anand? But how would she reach England? She did not know the answers to any of the questions that plagued her.

Anupama was no longer allowed to do any work in the house and she began to feel humiliated and suffocated. The whole town was probably talking about her now. Sundarakka would have spread the news faster than the speed of light, and Anupama was sure people were saying all kinds of things.

'Did you know that Anupama has a white patch? Poor girl!' 'She thought she was a beauty queen. Serves her right!'

Anupama was worried about Anand as well. He was thousands of miles away from her. She was afraid Radhakka would convince him that she had had the white patch before their marriage. Would he believe her or his mother? He was the only one who knew that she had not had the patch at the time of their marriage.

Anand is not like these people. He is a doctor. Surely, he will persuade his mother to see reason, Anupama told herself repeatedly.

Each day felt like a year—there seemed to be no end to her torment. How could she carry on like this?

The end came very swiftly. The following morning, from her first floor room, Anupama saw Shamanna entering Lakshmi Nivas. She had not expected them to send for her father so soon.

Since Radhakka was already in the room, Anupama stood behind the door and watched as Shamanna took a seat on the edge of the sofa opposite her mother-in-law.

'I received your telegram last night. But as there is no night bus service from our village to the city, I had to take the first bus this morning. I apologize for the delay. Is everything all right with Anupama?'

'What can happen to her? She is hale and hearty.'

'Is there any news from Anand?'

'He is fine.'

'Is something wrong?' Shamanna was anxious to know why a telegram had been sent summoning him urgently.

'Nothing is wrong, apart than the fact that you deceived us and took advantage of our goodness. You are a poor schoolteacher, and your daughter looked so innocent. Dr Desai vouched for all of you and we believed him. In spite of being the groom's family, we conducted the wedding at our cost because our Anand said he liked Anupama. In return, you have given us a wonderful lesson in gratitude,' Radhakka commented sarcastically.

'Please tell me what happened. I can't understand what you're trying to tell me. If I have made any mistake, please forgive me. Anupama is very young. She is a motherless child. In case she has erred, kindly forgive her. Treat her like your own daughter. I will see to it that she behaves obediently, and you will have no reason to complain again. No doubt we are poor, but we have not tried to cheat you. God is our witness.'

'If so, call your witness to explain all that has happened. Your daughter had a white patch which you concealed so that Anand would marry her.'

Shamanna was shocked. 'What! Anu has a white patch? It is not true! Nobody in our family has ever had that disease. You must be mistaken.'

'Are you saying that I am lying? Then let me show you. Anupama!' Radhakka yelled.

Shamanna, too, called out for her. With a heavy heart and leaden steps, Anupama emerged from behind the door. Her father looked careworn, shocked and worried; her mother-in-law's face was calm and ruthless.

Speaking softly, Shamanna said, 'Anu, your mother-in-law says that you have a white patch. Is it true?'

Anupama did not reply. Her father repeated the question but still she remained silent.

Frustrated, he raised his voice, 'Anu, your mother-in-law is saying that we are liars. Tell me the truth!'

Anupama looked at her father and mother-in-law. She lifted her sari to show the patch as she spoke, 'Appa, there was nothing like this at the time of the marriage. This patch appeared only a month back. '

Radhakka looked triumphant, 'Take your daughter back with you; she need not come back until she's completely cured and my son returns and sends for her. We have been deceived, and I will inform Anand about this.' She turned towards Anupama and said, 'I hope you have understood what I've just said. Make sure you leave all the expensive gifts we have given you in your room, and take only what is yours when you go.'

Shamanna pleaded with Radhakka, 'Please have mercy on her. Don't punish her like this. You are her mother now.' With tears in his eyes he got up to touch her feet.

Knowing that Radhakka would humiliate him further, Anupama went up to her father and stopped him from falling at Radhakka's feet. 'Appa, don't demean yourself so much. I did not have this affliction before my marriage, and that's the truth. Wait here. . .I'll be back in a moment.'

Anupama went to her room, collected the few things that belonged to her, picked up one of Anand's photographs and returned where Shamanna waited for her. She took his hand in hers, and silently clutching her bag, walked out of the house. She knew in her heart that this was the last time she would be seeing the house or its people. . .but she did not look back even once.

—————

five

Sabakka had been pacing in and out of the house all morning. Radhakka's cryptic message had upset her greatly. In her heart of hearts, she knew that Anupama was not a troublemaker. But then why had her in-laws sent that telegram? She couldn't help but feel that something was seriously wrong.

It was noon when Sabakka saw her husband and Anupama coming towards the house in the scorching heat. Heaving a deep sigh, Shamanna quietly went and sat on the verandah outside the house. He looked drained and listless. Anupama walked inside without a word. Sabakka had no idea what was going on; she wanted to know why Anu had been sent home so unceremoniously. She waited for Shamanna to say something but he just leant back wearily against the wall.

'Why do you look so dejected? Has she quarrelled with her in-laws?'

There was no response.

'What is the matter with you?'

'I'm hungry,' Shamanna said at last. 'Go and get some food ready for us. I haven't had even a drop of water since the morning.'

'What kind of people are they? You went to visit them for the first time since the wedding and they didn't even offer you a glass of water? Look at Nanda's future in-laws! They are so kind and considerate. I told you right from the start to look for alliances within our social level. '

'Don't start now! I will speak to you later,' Shamanna's heart was heavy. He was worried about Anupama and he wanted to share his sorrows with a sympathetic companion who would say a few encouraging words. He was in no mood to deal with Sabakka's nagging.

Sabakka looked at Anupama carefully—her face was pale and her eyes swollen. So, she concluded, something had gone wrong between the girl and her in-laws. After lunch, Shamanna recounted the entire story to her.

Sabakka had never felt any affection for Anupama. The girl was a living reminder of her husband's first wife, the woman who had shared Shamanna's love before Sabakka entered his life. But in her heart she knew that Anupama would never cheat anyone. Sabakka was not bereft of compassion and all motherless children roused her sympathy, except Anupama. Unfortunately, Anu was beautiful and intelligent while her own daughters were not. And just when Sabakka had thought she was well rid of her, she had returned home in disgrace. Her Nanda's marriage talks could be affected by the scandal. How long was Anu going to stay with them? Would she remain there forever? The thought of seeing her face every day upset Sabakka even further.

'Why did you bring her here? You should have left her with her in-laws. They are rich and can afford her treatment. How long will she stay with us? You could have settled everything before coming here.'

'Why are you talking like that? How could I leave her there when they virtually threw her out of the house? It was my duty to bring her home. By the grace of God, if she is cured quickly, she can go back. We will inform Anand.

He is a doctor after all, he will arrange for her treatment.'

'This is a village. Everybody will ask us why Anupama has come back home, and the truth will soon come out. Once people find out that she has leukoderma, both my daughters' future will be at stake. And who knows when Anand will return?'

Shamanna did not know what to say. There was some truth in what Sabakka was saying, but as a father, how could he have left his daughter behind when her in-laws were being so cruel to her?

He said in a defeated voice, 'I will tell Anupama to write to Anand and ask him what should be done. Let her stay here in the meantime.'

Anupama could not help overhearing their conversation. She realized that Anand alone held the key to her future. She was also painfully aware that she had no money.

✃

There was no way she could call Anand from the village, so she decided to write to him instead and wait for his reply.

Dear Anand, she wrote

By now you must have heard the 'news' about me. But I want to tell you the truth.

The past two months have been the most terrifying of my life. It started with a live coal falling on my foot on Lakshmi puja. A few days after the wound healed, I noticed a small white patch there and since I did not know what to do about it, I consulted Dr Rao at the skin clinic in the city. He confirmed that it was leukoderma.

I am taking the treatment prescribed by Dr Rao. Please do not think that I hid this matter from your mother. I didn't tell anyone about my condition because I was scared and apprehensive. But your mother thinks that I have had the patch since before our marriage. She is convinced that

I hid it from you and tricked you into marrying me. But you know that is not true. I never even dreamt that you would want someone like me; I was always aware of the differences between us before you erased them.

Anand, you know I did not have the patch when we got married. Please tell your mother that I have not deceived you. I am staying with my father in the village. But how long can I stay here as an additional burden on my father?

Please make arrangements for me to join you as soon as possible. My thoughts are always with you.

I shall be waiting eagerly for your response.

Always yours,

Anu

৯

Life in the village was very hard for Anupama. Sabakka was an uneducated and old-fashioned woman who believed that white patches brought bad luck and were contagious. So, she treated Anupama with disdain and although Anupama tried her best to explain the nature of her ailment to Sabakka, she failed to convince her.

Days passed and there was no reply from Anand. At night, Anupama would sit by her window and gaze at the stars, wondering about Anand's reaction to her letter. He must have been upset; she realized that it would take some time for him to come to terms with what had happened. But Anupama was confident that he would reply to her soon.

Papanna told Anupama, 'You don't need to ask me every day. I know you are waiting for your husband's letter. The day I get it, I will bring it to you.'

By now, everyone in the village knew that Anupama had a white patch because of which her in-laws had sent her back, and that her husband had not written to her.

There were many rumours about it. Malicious stories, which had not even a semblance of truth, spread through the village, and Anupama could not help hearing the whispered gossip. The villagers asked Sabakka all sorts of questions about her.

'How come Anupama is here? It is not the festive season. . .' Or, 'Is Anupama in the family way that she has come home?' Or, 'We have not seen anyone from her in-laws' family come to your place.'

Sabakka would struggle with her lies. 'Oh, she has just come here for a change. She's going to England to join her husband in a few months.'

Through all this, hidden from everyone, the white patch on Anupama's foot kept spreading. The more it spread, the lower Anupama's spirits sank. The medicines that she was taking regularly did not have any effect on the patch. Months passed, and still there was no news from Anand. At first Anupama had thought that the letter had got lost and Anand had not received it. So she wrote a few more letters, but still there was no reply.

At last, Papanna came by the house to deliver a letter for Anupama. She ran to the door, ecstatic, Anand had not forgotten her! He was going to honour the vows he had made at the time of their wedding.

But when she saw the ordinary inland letter, Anupama's hopes plummeted. It was from Sumithra. Bravely swallowing her tears, she went inside and opened the letter.

It carried good news. Sumithra was getting married and the boy's name was Hari Prasad. He was a sales engineer in Bombay, and Sumithra insisted that Anupama attend the wedding.

For a moment she forgot her own troubles in her happiness for Sumithra. And then she realized that she

Sudha Murty

could not go for the wedding. It would only give people an opportunity to talk about her.

She remembered a day, long ago, when she had dropped in unexpectedly at Sumithra's house. They were hoping to finalize an alliance for Sumithra, and her mother had been extremely upset to see Anupama. She felt that with Anupama there, Sumi was sure to be rejected. Then, her beauty had threatened her best friend's happiness. Now, her skin problem would cast a shadow over the ceremony, for she was sure some of the orthodox people there would say, 'Why did you invite this girl for such an auspicious occasion?'

Anupama did not have the strength to cope with such stinging remarks. Though Sumi was like a sister to her, she decided not to attend the wedding. But later that night, she prayed for Sumi's happiness: *Let your husband be a man who will only shower happiness and love on you. It is better to have an understanding husband than one who is merely handsome and wealthy. Marriage is a gamble. The result cannot be predicted beforehand. Finding the right match is a matter of chance. I was unlucky in this. May you be more fortunate.*

Anupama mused. . .sooner or later her sisters would also get married and go away to start their own families. They would have a companion to share their joys and sorrows, and they would have children. But her own life would be as silent as a graveyard. She wondered where she had gone wrong. Why was she being punished? Was there no escape from this ordeal? It seemed as though even God had turned a deaf ear to her prayers.

There was still no word from Anand.

Was he, perhaps, too unwell to write? Or, had he sent his reply to Radhakka's address? Should she ask Radhakka to redirect all her letters to the village? No, that would be a futile exercise. But then she remembered that in her letters to Anand she had written the correct return address at the back of the envelope. She thought of Dr Desai who had brought them together. Though he was now in Delhi he would certainly know where Anand was and what he was doing. Should she subject herself to the humiliation of asking a third person for her husband's address? Anupama was well aware that the relationship between husband and wife was an intensely private one. But now, circumstances had forced her to ask an outsider for help. Anupama cast aside her doubts and wrote to Dr Desai.

Late one evening, when Anupama was alone at home, there was a knock on the door. Sabakka had gone to the temple, her father had gone to the market, and her sisters were at a neighbour's house to attend some function. Anupama was only too aware that she was no longer welcome on auspicious occasions, and even when people invited her she refrained from going anywhere.

When Anupama opened the door, she saw two men standing outside. They looked Anupama up and down, as if they were examining her, and she felt extremely uncomfortable. 'Please come inside. Appa will be returning any minute now,' she said, and brought them some water to drink.

The older of the two asked her, 'Are you the eldest daughter?'

'Yes,' she replied. When the strangers did not say anything further, she went into the kitchen.

When Sabakka returned home and saw the visitors, she grew visibly excited. She went inside and asked Anupama, 'What did you offer them? Do you know who they are?

They are our Nanda's prospective in-laws!' She happily hurried away to prepare some snacks for them.

Anupama slipped away to her room, knowing that Sabakka would not want her around the guests.

Shamanna arrived a few minutes later with Nanda and Vasudha in tow. Nanda quietly went to help her mother in the kitchen.

'I'm sorry I was not at home to receive you properly. We did not know you were coming today. Please stay with us tonight. I wanted to meet you earlier and fix the date of the marriage, but there were some problems and I was held up. What will you have—tea or coffee?'

The old man gestured to him to stop. The other person who was his brother said, 'Masterji, we just happened to be in the neighbourhood, so we came to see you. We cannot stay for dinner as we have to go back soon.'

They had tea and Shamanna then accompanied them to the bus-stop.

Sabakka spent the next few days preparing for her daughter's wedding. Her standard response to anything that needed to be done for Anupama's wedding had always been, 'It is beyond our reach.' But for Nanda's wedding, she did not spare any expense. Anupama sighed. She had found a husband who was far above anything she had aspired for. But he had slipped out of her reach.

⇜

A few days later, Papanna brought two letters, one for Anupama and the other for Shamanna. Dr Desai had written to tell her that he had been to England the previous month, and had met Anand there. When Anupama saw the address Dr Desai had given, she was shocked. It was the same address to which she had written all her letters. The implication was all too clear—Anand must have received her letters but had chosen not to reply.

Anupama turned to see what her father was doing. Shamanna had collapsed after reading the letter that he had received. Anupama wondered what the letter said as she ran to get him some water.

The letter was from Nanda's prospective in-laws.

We had heard a rumour that your eldest daughter has leukoderma and because of that her husband has left her. We did not believe it and had come to see for ourselves. We now know that it was not a rumour but a fact. We do not want a daughter-in-law whose sister has white patches. As you are aware, ours is a very orthodox family and nobody will accept this alliance. . .Perhaps this alliance has not met with Lord Brahma's approval.

Please do not misunderstand us, but we are forced to call off the wedding.

The news came as a shock to everyone and Anupama bowed her head in shame. The grim silnce that swept through the house was broken by the sound of Nanda's sobs. Sabakka's anger erupted like a volcano; if she had possessed the power of Shiva's third eye, Anupama would have been reduced to ashes.

'It is because of her that they want to cancel the marriage. There is no point in weeping about this; you must go and inform them that Anupama and Nanda are stepsisters, not real sisters. Tell them that Anupama has inherited this affliction from her mother, and reassure them that they need have no worries about Nanda.'

Anupama knew that what Sabakka had said about her mother was not true. But if a harmless lie could help Nanda get married, she would not object. Anupama could not bear to see Nanda suffer because of her. She said in a low voice, 'Appa, please do as she says. If you can revive the alliance by doing that, no one will be happier than me.'

Shamanna was filled with despair, but he agreed to go the following morning. The household was in a state of nervous anticipation all day. Shamanna returned in the evening, looking downcast. They had told him bluntly, 'You are saying this because it suits you, but we don't want to take any chances with our son's future. We can always get a better alliance.'

Nanda's marriage was cancelled, and Anupama was blamed for this misfortune. This time Anupama did not weep—there were no more tears left inside her.

Shamanna seemed to age overnight; he became even quieter than before. Fate was conspiring against him, nothing was right in his life anymore. By the end of the month, he was transferred to another village, not unlike the one they were living in. Encouraged by this turn of events, Shamanna and his family soon settled down in the new village.

It had been a year since Anupama had returned to her father's house. Before moving to the new village, Anupama gave her new address to Papanna, and requested him to redirect her letters promptly. Even though she had realized otherwise, she still hoped that Anand would come for her one day. Since Shamanna was new to the village, no one had approached him for private tuitions yet. Life had become a struggle, and Sabakka vented all her frustrations and anger on Anupama. 'Your in-laws are rich. Why can't they send some money every month for your maintenance? It would have been better if you had stayed with them instead of coming here and adding to our burdens.'

But Anupama could not bring herself to add to her humiliation by asking her in-laws for money. Sabakka firmly believed that whatever they spent on Anupama was a sheer waste; she refused to acknowledge the fact that Anupama helped with the household chores all day long.

Anupama had wanted to take up a job as a teacher, but for that she needed a B.Ed. degree. So she resolved to go to the city—there she would start giving tuitions, and earn enough to study further.

If only she had contracted the skin ailment while she was at college, then Anand would not have married her and she would not have lost everything. She could have continued her education and taken up a job, casting aside all thoughts of marriage, instead of being a burden on her family.

A small white patch had ruined her career as well as her marriage.

As a student, she had always acted in plays that had a happy ending. She would tell Sumithra, 'I do not want to play the tragic heroine, Sumi. I want to show the audience the joy, the happiness, the magic transformation that love and beauty can bring. I believe in happy endings!'

But real life had proved to be different—she was learning the hard way that life is not always a fountain of happiness, but rather a mix of pain and sorrow. The drama of her life had only just begun, and she had no choice but to see it through to the end.

∽

Sumithra had moved to Bombay after her marriage. She knew about Anupama's problem and in one of her letters, she wrote,

Dear Anu,

I know you are extremely unhappy there and I want you to come and stay with us in Bombay for some time.

Instead of sitting at home and brooding over your fate in that village, come to this mega city. I am sure you will get a job; even I got one! I have discussed this with Hari; so you need not worry. Have courage and do not lose your patience.

Love, Sumi.

Do not lose your patience, Sumi had written, but how could Anupama not lose her patience when everyone around her treated her with such contempt? The only thing that was keeping her despair from overwhelming her was the determination to overcome all her misfortunes without ever giving in.

Savantri, the school ayah, would leave the school keys every day in Shamanna's house. One evening, she took Anupama aside and said, 'Can I suggest something to you?'

'What?'

'Our village goddess is very powerful. She never rejects a sincere devotee's prayer. If you worship her with white flowers every morning for twenty-one days your disease will disappear.'

'Savantri, I have prayed to many gods and goddesses in various temples. I have gone to dargahs and churches, but nothing has helped me.'

Savantri persevered, 'This is a different goddess. Why can't you try?'

Anupama kept quiet. Despite the cures that people suggested for her condition every now and then, it was spreading quietly and inexorably.

Shamanna and Sabakka were discussing Nanda's future. 'If you carry on doing nothing about it, my daughters will die unmarried. Why aren't you trying to find husbands for them?' Sabakka urged her husband.

'Who says I am not trying? I have met Vishwanath's family four times already. They said they would let us know within a few days whether they are interested in pursuing the alliance, but I have still to hear from them.'

'What about Kulkarni's family?'

'They are even worse than Vishwanath. They told me straightaway that they knew why the earlier engagement was broken off, and they do not want an alliance with our family.'

'This is all because of Anupama,' muttered Sabakka.

Shamanna was tired of all the troubles that had beset him. He said in a pained voice, 'Why did I have to father girls? They have become millstones around my neck. My worries have doubled since Anu returned home Why does she have to remain here? I am going to retire soon; how will I fend for all of us?'

⁂

Shamanna's words had pierced Anupama's heart like a hot skewer. She constantly tried to find ways to reduce her father's burden, but to no avail. She sometimes wished the ground beneath her feet would split open and swallow her. But she was no Sita, born of the earth, to be taken back into its folds; she was the ordinary daughter of a poor schoolteacher.

There was only one option left for her. She would pray— one last time—to the goddess of the village as Savantri had suggested. She thought of the innumerable shrines she had visited, the many types of medicines she had tried, the saints she had prayed to, and the vows she had taken. Would the village goddess be the one to help her? She did not know, but she was so desperate for a cure that she was prepared to try anything. The next morning, she got up early, took a bath and collected the white flowers for her visit to the temple.

While combing her hair, Anupama looked into the mirror and shivered with shock. A small white patch had appeared on her arm. It was the death knell for her happiness; a sign that she should abandon all hopes of a cure. She felt as if she had caught a thief stealthily entering the house. The patches would spread rapidly over the rest of her body. . .and the doors of her mother-in-law's house would remain shut forever.

Tears blurred her vision as sorrow welled up in her heart. What was the point in going to the temple now? She started sobbing, but there was not a soul to console her. She was like a lonely traveller on a long and arduous road.

Anupama heard her father stir. She didn't want him to know that she was crying, so she took the flowers that she had plucked, and silently walked out of the house.

The temple of the goddess of the village was on top of a hillock two kilometres from the house. At that hour of the morning, the only people out were the devotees who were going to the temple. Exhausted, Anupama slowly made her way up the path, completely oblivious of her surroundings. It was a while before she noticed the two women walking ahead of her. They were talking so loudly that Anupama could hear them without any difficulty.

'Sharada, why did you take this vow?' the older woman asked her companion.

'My husband had some problems at office. His boss is very strict and wants to transfer him. Someone told me that if I prayed to the goddess and offered her a sari, the transfer would be cancelled.'

'Oh, I never knew the goddess was so powerful.'

Even in her present state of dejection, Anupama smiled ruefully. Could the goddess satisfy everyone's wishes—cure her white patches, cancel a transfer, grant children to the childless, and who knew what else? How could the goddess fulfil such endless desires?

The conversation went on.

'Indira, by the way, you never told me anything about the wedding.'

'Oh, it was fabulous. Girija looked like the goddess Lakshmi herself. And the groom. . .he is so handsome! He works at a very high position in his office. Radhakka is truly blessed, but for one thing.'

'They have Lakshmi's blessings, what problems can they possibly have?'

'Life is never perfect, Sharada. God gives everyone their share of woes, otherwise they'll stop thinking about Him. In Radhakka's case it is her son, Anand.'

Anupama's breath caught when she heard Anand's name and, for a moment, she forgot her own worries as she waited for the older woman to continue.

'It seems he fell in love with and married a very poor but beautiful girl.'

'Have you seen her?'

'No. I couldn't go for the wedding as there was some problem at home. It seems Anand liked the girl so much that her father took advantage of it, and Radhakka had to perform the wedding at her own expense.'

'How fortunate for the girl's family!' sneered the younger woman.

'The story does not end there. The girl had white patches, which she had hidden from everyone. The moment Radhakka found out, she sent the daughter-in-law packing. Now she is searching for a new bride for Anand.'

Sudha Murty

'Has he agreed to that?'

'Of course. Otherwise why would Radhakka search for a bride? The first time, they brought home a bride from an unknown family, and look what happened. She doesn't want to be deceived again. So, this time, she is looking for an alliance within her own circle.'

Anupama was shocked. Till that moment, a part of her had been sure that Anand still loved her and had good reasons for not writing to her. The fact that he had agreed to remarry meant that he was prepared to discard her like a rag and move on with his life. So, when he had talked about being together 'till death do us part' his words had held no truth. Anupama had essayed many roles on stage— Samyukta, Vasavadatta, Noor Jahan and countless others. She would get so immersed in the characters that, long after the plays had been staged, she would still remember the dialogues. But Anand, who had never been on stage, had surpassed her in real life! Anand was a doctor; he knew more about the 'disease' than most people. Then why was he behaving in such a manner? What would he have done if his mother or his sister had fallen prey to the affliction? Would he have deserted them as he had her? He would probably have sympathized with them and taken care of them, but when it was his own wife, the woman he claimed to love, he had abandoned her. The rules were different. . .and society would not question his behaviour. But then, his family had never experienced a problem such as this; they did not know the meaning of suffering or poverty. They could not imagine the difficulties, the sorrow and the despair of someone in her position.

Anupama was jolted out of her thoughts by Sharada's voice.

'But has he divorced his first wife?'

'Oh, they've been separated for the last three years. That is not a problem. She is from a poor family. Radhakka will pay her some money, and that will be the end of the matter. She has nobody to support her, so she won't have the courage to fight her in-laws. When the girl's husband is not bothered about her, why should anybody else care? Sharda, do you know of any good girl?'

'I don't know anyone. Besides, I've heard that Radhakka can be very domineering, so I don't want to recommend anybody. And, after all, this will be a second marriage. By the way, how is Anand to look at?'

'Oh, he is such a handsome boy, but obviously very unlucky. I feel sorry for him. He has come for his sister's wedding and will be going back soon.'

Anand had come to India but had not even bothered to contact her! How could he have been so heartless? Anupama suddenly felt very tired and her steps faltered. She was in two minds—should she go to the temple and offer her prayers, or just return home? Could the goddess do anything for her any more? As the sun rose behind the hill and its warm rays began to dissipate the fog, Anupama turned her thoughts to her future. There was really nobody who loved her enough to bother about her.

As a little girl, she had never known her mother's affection. Her father, who had no self-confidence, was a puppet in the hands of his second wife. Only her grandmother loved her, but after her death Anupama had grown up unwanted. Meeting Anand brought joy in her life again. She thought he had showered all his love on her, and she too had loved him in return.

She suddenly realized that she had reached the top of the hill. The entire village spread out below her. Near the temple was a ledge that overlooked a deep valley. If anyone

Sudha Murty

jumped from there, they would definitely die. The temple authorities had hung a board warning people not to go there.

Anupama sat down on a stone outside the temple. What did she have to look forward to? Nothing! As long as she lived, she would have to face hundreds of problems; and she would be a burden on her father, and a bane for her sisters. Sabakka's taunts would only add to her misery. Anupama could see only one way to solve all her problems. She gazed at the ledge—it was only a few steps away, and death was waiting. What it required now was a little courage—after all, what did she have to live for? The more she thought about it, the more appealing it seemed. She could imagine what people would say. 'Oh, poor Anupama, she had a white patch, so she killed herself.' Or, 'The unfortunate girl slipped from the hill.' Or, 'Poor girl, her husband rejected her, what else could she do?' Or, 'Her husband left her. She must have had an affair and got into trouble. So she committed suicide. How shameful!'

But how would it matter once she was dead? Nothing would hurt her. Would anybody feel sorry for her? Miss her? Her father would probably shed a few tears and then forget about her. That was only natural. Sumi would definitely feel sad and weep for a while. But she had her own family, and Anupama would soon become just a memory. Anand? He would feel relieved once she was gone.

Her mind was made up now. But still she couldn't bring herself to move. Some unseen power was holding her back. Anupama thought of Girija and her loose morals. With money and her mother's support, she had married into a rich family and was a respected member of society. In conduct, looks and disposition, Anupama was better than Girija, but a small white patch was pushing her to her death. Was this fair? It was not her fault that she had white patches. Then why did she have to die? Even if she died, no one would care. Society at large would take Anand's side and sympathize with him.

She had finally discovered the real Anand. He had loved her beauty and married her for it. He was not ready to accept her if her beauty was in any way marred. People would pity him and that would be unbearable for him.

Why should she die for a husband who didn't even care about her? Though he had talked about a union that only death could sunder, it was a small white patch that had parted them!

He had taken his marriage vows in front of hundreds of people, in the presence of Agni. Yet, he had betrayed her and the commitment he had made to her.

She recalled a line from one of her plays, 'Why did God give strong arms and the courage of a lion to man?' 'So that he can rescue helpless women, the distressed, and the forsaken,' was the reply. But Anand had failed to rise to the occasion and come to her aid.

Naturally, one should respect one's mother. But when she was wrong, was it not the duty of the son to stand up to her and tell her that she had made a mistake? Anupama realised, for the first time, that Radhakka and Anand were very similar. The only difference was their gender and age. Anand was obedient because he did not have the courage to stand up to his mother. Also, because he himself was just like her!

Anupama's thoughts were racing. She was beginning to feel uncomfortable with the decision she had made. She was practical enough to realize that what she was contemplating was not the correct solution. What would happen if she jumped but did not die? She could be crippled for life, and would be worse off than she was now. Her decision would not make it any easier for her sisters to get married or reduce her father's burdens. Anupama calmed herself and decided to return home.

She looked down at the valley again, and saw it in a different light. The sun had risen higher; there were numerous wild flowers getting ready to blossom; birds were flying out from their nests in search of food. Life had begun to have new meaning for her.

Anupama climbed down the steps. Whatever the circumstances she found herself in, she would meet the challenge head-on, and win. She was now ready to face the world, determined to stand on her own feet and build a new life for herself. She looked back and prayed to the goddess, *Give me the courage to live no matter what happens!* and started walking home.

Shamanna was engrossed in writing something when Anupama walked up to him and said, 'Appa, I am getting bored here. I want to go to Bombay and stay with Sumi.'

Her voice was bold and firm. Shamanna raised his head in surprise and asked her, 'When will you be back?'

'I do not know. Maybe, after a few months.' She knew in her heart of hearts that she would never come back.

A nupama stepped onto the platform at Dadar railway station, feeling anxious and tense. She had never been to Bombay before, and was flabbergasted by the huge crowds. For a moment she wondered whether it had been a mistake to bank on Sumi's help alone, now that she had decided to take such a big step. She had come to this unknown city with just a small suitcase of clothes and some of her favourite books. As she stood irresolute on the platform, she saw Sumi and felt waves of relief wash over her.

'Sumi! I am so glad to see you. Bombay scares me.'

'Which is why I thought I'd come to the station to receive you. I'm on leave today,' Sumithra said as she led Anupama to board a local train.

Everything was new for Anupama—the language, the people, the sultriness of the air. . .everything. She stuck close to her friend until they reached Versova where Sumithra had a tiny single-bedroom apartment. Accustomed as she was to the wide-open spaces of the village, Anupama found the flat and its surroundings congested, although it had all the modern conveniences.

Sumithra worked six days a week, with Sunday off. Her husband was an engineer, and his weekly holiday was on Thursday. 'Anu, you've stopped taking care of yourself in the three years since your wedding. Now that you are here, you must treat this as your home. I want you to relax here; we'll look after you,' Sumithra's voice was charged with emotion.

Anupama was so overwhelmed by her friend's affection that she could hardly speak. No one had spoken to her so tenderly for a long time.

'Sumi, please try to get me a job as soon as possible. I have been idle for the last three years, and I am going mad. Appa has a lot of financial worries and I must take up a job so that I can support him.'

'Don't worry. I will talk to Hari. He will help you. Anu, isn't it Anand's duty to send you some money to support you? Can't Dr Desai tell him this at least?'

'Sumi, I do not want money from someone who doesn't love me. God will provide for me. I have my education, and it will serve to feed me.'

'Anu, your mother-in-law is so religious and god-fearing. Doesn't she know that these things will be useless if the basic quality of humanity is absent? How can she treat you so badly?' Sumithra's anger rose with every word, before Anupama calmed her down.

'Sumi, let's not talk about them. I want to look ahead rather than remain stuck in the past.'

'Okay. What kind of a job do you want? You're far too intelligent to be an ordinary clerk like me.'

'Sumi, what I like or dislike is not important. I cannot afford to be choosy. Any job is fine by me!'

'I feel terrible about this. You were so fond of plays and literature when we were studying. A person like you should be a lecturer in a college.'

Anupama laughed. 'Forget all that now. My life has become a play now.'

They had their lunch and Anupama, who was tired after the journey, slept for a while. When she woke up, she heard Sumithra talking to her husband, Hari. She felt a little awkward because of her situation, but nevertheless greeted him with a smile.

'Anu, this is Hari Prasad, that is, Mr Sumithra!'

Hari was surprised when he saw her. From Sumi's description, he had imagined Anupama as an ordinary girl with white patches marring her face and body. But the girl he saw standing before him was breathtakingly beautiful; she was like a heavenly vision come down to earth. Compared to Anupama, Sumithra looked plainer than ever before.

He greeted Anupama politely. Anupama's smile faltered in the face of Hari's worshipful gaze. Many boys would look at her with the same expression during her college days. But she calmed herself; once the patches appeared on her face things would be quite different.

'I want to thank you for letting me stay with you. Sumi said you would help me get a job in Bombay.'

'Oh, that will not be a problem. Since this is your first trip to Bombay, why don't you do some sightseeing first? Take a look at the Elephanta Caves, Victoria Terminus, Borivili Park, and so on. Please make yourself comfortable in our house.'

Although Hari's words reassured Anupama, she continued to feel somewhat apprehensive. Sumithra was her friend, but how would Hari feel if she continued to stay there for some length of time?

A month passed. She and Sumithra had visited a few places in and around Bombay, and Hari too had accompanied them on occasion. Though he was very nice to her, Anupama was always conscious that she was a guest in their house, and felt that it would be best if she moved out as soon as possible.

Sudha Murty

Hari and Sumithra would leave for the office early in the morning and return late in the evening. Anu would finish all the household work in the meantime. In her free time, she would sit on Versova beach and let her thoughts wander.

One day Hari came home in high spirits. 'Anupama, I have a friend called Gopal Athrey. It seems there is a vacancy in his office for a clerk. . If you're interested, we can go for an interview tomorrow.'

Anupama smiled, 'That is excellent news.'

'But you'll have to travel to the Fort area every day.'

'So many people commute, why should I be an exception?'

The following day, Anupama went to Mr Athrey's office. She was anxious to get the job so that she would no longer be a burden on Sumi. 'Please, God,' she prayed, 'please let me get this job somehow.'

She waited in the visitors' room and watched as the receptionist pulled out a small mirror from her purse and touched up her lipstick. Anupama had never used any make-up, except for a few light touches while acting in plays. She believed that it was not the make-up but the expression and modulation of voice that breathed life into the character that she played. She wondered where all her hopes and dreams had gone. Even in her bleakest moments, she had never seen herself looking for a job as a clerk.

Her musings were cut short when the receptionist, Dolly, asked, 'Are you Anupama?'

Anupama nodded, and was asked to go in.

There were three people inside. The senior-most of them told her, 'Your qualifications are very impressive, but this is a clerical post. It involves a lot of repetitive work. If you are sure you want to take it up, you can join tomorrow.'

Anupama was very happy. She thanked them and left.

'Poor girl!' Gopal Athrey said.

'What do you mean? She is so beautiful and intelligent.'

'My friend, Hari, was telling me that she has leukoderma and that her husband has left her.'

'But we could not see any patches.'

'Anyway, it does not concern us as long as she is efficient. If you look carefully, everyone has some problem or the other. We should not bother about such things.'

❧

Anupama's eyes filled with tears of joy when she received her first salary. She considered it her duty to send some money to her father. She even offered Sumithra money to cover her expenses, but it was Hari who stopped her, saying, 'How can I take money from you? If I had my sister staying with me, would I take money from her? You are just like a sister to me. You can stay in our house as long as you wish.'

With financial independence, Anupama's confidence began to blossom. She had become friends with many of the girls who worked with her. They were from various backgrounds and even different regions of the country, and they lived in different parts of Bombay. None of them ever talked about her skin patches or her past. Anupama, too, had begun to accept her condition and look beyond it. The darkest period of her life was behind her now. She and Dolly travelled to and from work together every day, and they became good friends over a period of time.

Anupama constantly felt the need to take up accommodation of her own. Sumi and Hari were very cordial with her, but she was afraid that such closeness could end in unhappiness.

Sudha Murty

She had requested all her friends to help her find a place to stay. But, so far, she had not been able to find anything that was within her means.

When Anupama received her Deepavali bonus, she bought a silk sari for Sumi and a silver bowl for Hari. As she gave them the gifts, Hari objected, saying that they were too expensive. Anupama silenced him by saying, 'This is a gift from your sister for Deepavali.' She was deeply grateful for the way they had helped her in her time of need.

᷾

One day, Dolly did not come to office. As she was engaged and was emigrating to Australia after marriage, Anupama thought that she was perhaps busy with her preparations for the wedding. But when she called up her house, she was told that Dolly had met with an accident and that she had been hospitalized. Anupama immediately applied for leave and rushed to the hospital. Outside the hospital room, Dolly's ageing mother, Mary, sat crying, surrounded by a few friends. Most of her family was in Goa, and Dolly was her only daughter.

When Anupama met the doctor to find out if anything was required, he said, 'Your friend needs blood. These days the incidence of AIDS is so high that we prefer blood from a known person. Perhaps one of the relatives can help? Dolly has lost a lot of blood; she needs a transfusion as soon as possible.'

The moment they heard that blood was needed, Dolly's visitors quietly melted away. Anupama told the doctor, 'Doctor, if my blood group is compatible with hers, I am ready to give my blood.' She hesitated for a moment, 'I suffer from leukoderma—will it affect her in any way?'

'Of course not! Leukoderma cannot be passed on through blood transfusions.'

Anupama belonged to the same blood group as Dolly. After giving the blood, she went and met Dolly's mother and persuaded her to go home, promising to stay with Dolly through the night. She did not say anything about having donated her blood.

Until Dolly left the hospital, Anupama stayed with her every night to help her. Dolly was overwhelmed with gratitude. Holding Anupama's hand, she said, 'Anu, how can I ever thank you for all that you've done for me?'

Anupama interrupted her, 'Don't talk as though I've done something great. You needed some blood and I was able to give it to you. That's all.'

෴

Chandrika, one of Anupama's colleagues at the office, was getting married, and Anupama had taken half a day off to attend the wedding. She knew it would be quite unlike the small-town weddings she had attended so far where the festivites often went on for three days. Chandrika's wedding would be a short and simple ceremony. Anupama was very excited about attending it; after a long time, she'd again taken an interest in dressing up. She went to the Dadar market and bought a silver bowl before rushing off to the wedding hall.

It was an unostentatious wedding. Anupama sat in a corner and observed all that was going on. Unbidden, her thoughts went back to her own wedding. What a display of wealth and grandeur! How much money had been spent on the hall, flowers, decorations and the catering! She felt as though it had all been a dream. What was the use of all that expense? The real success of a marriage depended not on superficial factors such as those, but upon love and mutual understanding between husband and wife.

After the wedding lunch, Anupama went straight home. She'd assumed that the house would be locked as usually, at that time of the day, everyone was at work. But to her surprise she found Hari at home.

Anupama kept her purse on the table and asked, 'How come you're home?'

Hari smiled at her and answered, 'I am going away on tour today, and I came to collect my baggage.'

Anupama did not think there was anything unusual about that as Hari was in the sales department. She went into the bedroom and shut the door behind her, but did not lock it. She started to change out of her new sari when, suddenly, she felt a pair of hands grasping her from behind. She immediately realized who it was and was terrified. She did not know what to do. With great difficulty she turned around, and saw Hari smiling at her. He thought Anupama looked stunning in her new sari. Anupama was extremely angry but Hari thought she looked even more beautiful in her anger.

'Hari, how could you do such a thing?' Anupama stammered.

'Anupama, your beauty has fascinated me from the moment I first saw you. All I see in my dreams is you. Why are you waiting for your foolish husband? Do you think he will ever come back to you? You are wasting your youth instead of enjoying it. Anu, we can be together without anyone ever coming to know about it. I will protect you, whatever the circumstances.'

Anupama was so angry now that her face turned crimson, and she did not know what to say. Hari took her silence as consent, and he continued, 'Anu, compared to you, Sumi looks like a buffalo—I find her dull and unattractive. I have been waiting for so long to tell you how I feel, and today I found the opportunity. Anu, remember, I was the one who got you a job. Won't you thank me for it?'

Hari reached for Anupama again. But she gathered her courage and slapped his face hard.

'You should be ashamed of yourself. You have called me your sister. . .will you behave with your sister like this? I have always considered Sumi as my own sister and I will certainly tell her all about your edifying qualities. Get out of my way; I want to go out.'

Hari was stunned, but he continued to stand, leaning against the door. 'Just because I say you are my sister you can't become my sister. I said that to mislead Sumi. I had never even met you before, how can you become my sister? Anu, you do remember that you have leukoderma, don't you? Anand will never come back to you, nor will anyone else want to marry you. Let us not waste our time arguing when we could find such pleasure in each other's company. No one will ever suspect us.'

'Let me go!' Anupama shouted.

'Anu, you are as hungry for the pleasures of marital life as I am. If you don't agree to do as I say, I will turn Sumi against you. I'll convince her that you were chasing me. She will believe her husband over her friend, any day.'

The loud knock on the door momentarily distracted Hari. Seizing the chance, Anupama flew like a hunted deer and opened the door. A middle-aged saleswoman stood outside. 'Madam, our company manufactures liquid soap. It is not well known in the market because we can't afford to advertise, but if you clean anything with our soap. . .'

Sudha Murty

Under normal circumstances, Anupama would have refused, but today she felt that God had sent this woman to her rescue. She called her inside. 'Please sit down,' she said, taking twenty rupees from her purse. 'Give me one bottle.'

The saleswoman was very happy. Apologetically she said, 'I don't have any change.'

'Oh! It doesn't matter!' said Anupama. Relieved, she walked out of the house with the saleswoman.

Hari just stood there, powerless to stop her.

Anupama went to Versova beach and sat down there. She was in a state of shock. It was a hot and humid day; very few people were on the beach. Anupama began to cry uncontrollably. She felt as if she had been climbing a sheer mountain face clinging to a rope for help, and then found that the rope had turned into a snake. She felt herself falling...

She experienced the same sense of desolation and despair that she had felt when she had first noticed the white patch on her body, and was assailed by fear and pain. What would she do now? How could she continue to stay with Sumi? Where else could she go in that huge bustling city? Anupama's senses were numb and her mind blank. She thought of Anand; he was responsible for her suffering. He had abandoned her when she needed him the most. And Hari, whom she had looked upon as an elder brother, had hurt her terribly by his actions. His words still echoed in her mind, causing her fresh pain. It seemed that even God had forsaken her. Did He have no one else to torture and test?

The sun was setting and many young couples had come to the beach to enjoy the evening breeze. Anupama suddenly realized she had been sitting there for more than six hours. She had to go back now. She mustered her courage, and reluctantly traced her steps home.

Sumi was cooking when Anupama entered the flat. As soon as she saw Anupama's pale cheeks, swollen eyes and sad face, she exclaimed, 'Anu, what happened? Are you not well? How was the wedding?'

Anupama did not reply.

'Go and rest for a while. I'll finish cooking in an hour. Hari is out of station; he left a note saying he will return in a week.'

Anupama inferred from Sumi's behaviour that she was unaware of what had happened. She went inside with a heavy heart, and lay down on her bed. Sumi went back to the kitchen, *Anupama is probably sad because the wedding reminded her of her own marriage.*

৺

The following morning Anupama went to Dolly's house on her way to work, and found her busy applying her make-up.

'Anu, what a pleasant surprise! How come you're here so early? Is everything all right?'

Anupama did not know what to say. The previous day's incident had shocked her, but she could not tell anyone about it. She closed the door and started crying, 'Dolly, can you please get me a room in a working women's hostel? I want it within a week.'

Anupama wanted to shift out before Hari returned from his tour.

'Anu, what happened? Why are you in such a state?'

'Dolly, please don't ask me anything. I can't afford paying-guest accommodation in a city like Bombay. But you know so many people. . .please help me somehow.'

'Anu, I'm sure I can find you accommodation with some Goan Christian family. But why don't you stay here? My mom and I are the only people here; you could live in the spare room outside. You'll have to cook your own food, though, as we are non-vegetarians.'

Anupama was delighted. Dolly's mother owned a small colonial-style bungalow with a fairly large garden in Bandra. It had been given to her long ago, at the time of her marriage, when real estate prices had not been astronomical. The house was in a somewhat run-down state. Many builders, who wished to demolish it and build a shopping complex or residential apartments, were pressurizing Dolly's mother to sell the house but she was not willing to sell the property.

Accommodating Anupama for a short period was not a problem for Dolly.

'Dolly, I don't know how to thank you,' Anupama said gratefully.

৯

Hari returned home after a week, and found Sumi cooking dinner. The house was quiet. He noticed that the table had been laid for two. 'Why have you put out only two plates? Where is Anupama?' he asked his wife.

'Oh! She left this morning. She got a PG accommodation in Bandra. I did try to persuade her to wait until your return but she said she would meet you at your office later. I'll miss her a lot but in a way it's good that she moved out before my delivery. With my mother coming to help me with the baby, it would have been difficult to accommodate us all.'

Hari was very upset. 'Why didn't you insist that she stay with us a little longer?' he almost shouted.

Sumithra answered calmly, 'Hari, try to understand. You already helped by getting her a job. She lived with us for almost a year. Don't you think I felt bad when she left? But in life partings are inevitable. I know she was like a sister to you, but even if she had been your own sister, she couldn't have stayed with us forever. Anupama is a very sensitive person; she would not have been comfortable staying with us indefinitely. I've told her that she is always welcome here.'

Hari was still upset and lashed out at Sumi, 'You are a terrible cook. This food is unpalatable.' He washed his hands in the plate and got up.

Sumi could not understand why Hari was being so difficult. She tried to mollify him. 'I'm sorry. I must have added chilli twice. Let me bring you some sugar and lime. Don't be upset, please.'

She had no way of knowing that the root cause of the problem was not the chilli powder, but something quite different. Hari knew very well that Anupama would never enter his house again when he was around, or meet him at his office.

As for Anupama, the days were carefree and she enjoyed herself as much as she could. She and Dolly got along extremely well, and through her she met many people in different walks of life. Lately, however, Anupama had started getting bored at the office. Her job as a clerk did not nurture her talent and creativity and was not challenging enough for her. She had begun to feel the need for a change, but she could not afford to leave her job.

One day Dolly said to her, 'Anu, there is a vacancy for a Sanskrit lecturer at a college in Vile Parle. Father Sebastian is the principal there. Remember, you met him at our Christmas party? Why don't you apply for the post?'

'How can I? I don't have any experience in teaching.'

'But you know the language well, and that should help. And it doesn't say anywhere that you can't apply just because you aren't experienced. I will also speak to Father Sebastian.'

Anupama went to the interview hesitantly. Apparently, there were very few candidates for the post. There were three people on the interview panel, including Father Sebastian. They were impressed by her academic record. One of them asked, 'Anupama, your certificates vouch for your academic excellence. But you've been working as a clerk for the last year. One would have thought that with your qualification you would have opted for research or for a teaching job. Why did you choose to do a clerical job?'

Anupama hesitated, and then, in a low tone, she replied, 'I had some personal problems.'

Father Sebastian explained the nature of the job. 'This is not going to be just a lecturer's job. Our college has a very good cultural centre. We are looking for someone who will make the students aware of our culture, and motivate them to participate in intercollegiate events; someone who is familiar with Sanskrit plays, and is willing to participate in our theatre programmes. Our college is fairly big, so you will have to work really hard.'

Anupama was overjoyed. 'Certainly, Father! I would love to direct the plays.' Anupama no longer hoped to play the role of a heroine—the white patches now covered her hands as well.

~

Dolly's wedding was a big event. It took place in the Bandra Church with all her cousins from Goa and Australia in attendance. After the wedding, Dolly's mother went to Goa, and Dolly left with her husband for Melbourne.

Over the past few months, Anupama had become a part of their family, and Dolly's eyes brimmed with tears when she said goodbye to Anupama. 'Anu, my mother and I don't want to sell this house or get a builder to develop it, right now. This bungalow has been with our family for ages, and we want to retain it as long as possible. I don't trust my cousins, but I have complete faith in you. Please stay here as long as you want and look after it. You needn't give me any rent.'

It was unbelievable! No documents were to be signed, and no money was exchanged. Based on faith alone, Dolly was entrusting her with their precious home! Anupama agreed enthusiastically. 'Dolly, the house will always be waiting for you. Whenever you want me to leave, just tell me in advance,' she said as she bid Dolly goodbye.

Anu was sad for a while after she left her old job and joined the college. She missed her colleagues, but as a lecturer she soon became confident and self-assured. She had removed her mangalsutra—it had weighed down on her heavily, in more ways than one.

Without being conscious of it, a visit to the seashore to gaze at the waves had become a part of Anupama's daily routine. She loved wandering along the Bandra seashore, watching the endless waves smash tirelessly against the black rocks, oblivious to everything else.

Sumi gave birth to a baby boy. Hari was transferred to Kolhapur a few weeks later. Anupama went to see Sumi and the baby before they left, and gave the baby a gold chain. Sumi was very happy to see her and whispered in the baby's ear, 'Look, your aunt has come to see you.'

Anupama shrank from the word 'aunt'. *I am not your aunt. I am just your mother's best friend.*

Bombay was being lashed by the fury of the monsoon. The sky was overcast, and the unrelenting downpour had cut off parts of the city. Dr Vasant wondered how high the water had risen in the vicinity, and peered out of the window.

He had been busy in the operation theatre since the morning. Emergency cases and his other duties had kept him so occupied that he had forgotten to have his lunch. It was almost time for dinner by the time he came back to his chambers. He could see Bombay Central station and its surging crowds in the distance. As usual, people were rushing to catch the local and outstation trains. The rain had brought great relief from the scorching heat of the summer, although it also created havoc, especially in the city's slums. Vasant bit hard on a small stone in the sabji halfway through his dinner, and winced. He was getting tired of eating the same thing every day—thick chapatis that were difficult to chew, curds with sugar, dal that was too oily, vegetable gravy with too much masala, and rice that had been cooked without the stones being picked out! He had been having the same dinner for so many years that he had started hating the thought of his evening meal. He yearned for his mother's cooking, but that was beyond his reach now.

Rainwater started streaming in from a broken window-pane. It formed a puddle and lapped against his feet. The cold rainwater reminded him of his childhood, of standing in the first shower after the hot summer. As children, they had believed that getting drenched in the first rains would bring them good luck and good health. But his mother, Tungakka, had not agreed with them. 'Vasant, come inside. Don't get wet. You will catch a cold.'

She had worried too much about diseases that never struck. But still, melting under his mother's love and care, he had always heeded her words and gone in.

The knock at the door interrupted his reminiscences. 'Yes, come in.'

'Doctor, an emergency case was just brought in,' the attendant announced without any emotion.

Vasant looked at his dinner plate and said, 'I will be there in a minute.' While he was washing his hands, the Bombay Central clock struck eight. He donned his white coat and headed for the emergency room. Sister Parvathi Ammu met him outside the ER. She looked at him and exclaimed in surprise, 'How come you are on duty again, doctor? Where is Doctor Satya?'

Vasant just smiled before walking into the ER.

Satya, like Vasant, was from Karnataka. They had known each other for the past three years, but their attitude to life was very different.

'Oh, Vasant! You don't know how to enjoy life. You should have been a sage! I'm on duty on Sunday, but I have some urgent work. How about an exchange? You stand in for me on Sunday and I'll take over your shift on Tuesday.'

He had not even waited for Vasant's reply. He had assumed that Vasant would agree, and merrily gone his way.

The Sunday duty exchange between them was quite common. Vasant knew very well what Satya meant by 'urgent work'. He would roam around with his junior, Dr Vidya, watch a movie at the Liberty or stroll down Marine Drive.

As soon as Vasant reached the ER, a police constable came up to him. 'Doctor, there has been an accident. This lady was crossing the road towards Bombay Central when a taxi jumped the red light and hit her. It was not her fault; she was at the zebra crossing. The taxiwala ran away but we caught up with him at the next signal and he is now in the lock-up.' The constable went on giving information that was in no way useful to Vasant.

Vasant was concentrating on the unconscious woman in front of him. She looked to be in her early twenties; her beautiful face was framed by long black hair. She had no ornaments on her. Her orange cotton sari was bloodstained, and blood still flowed from her injured leg. Vasant turned over her hand to examine it and noticed the white patches. For a moment he thought, *What a blemish on this beautiful portrait!*

And then, as the doctor within him took over, he proceeded to ascertain the extent of her injuries. He soon became so engrossed in treating her that he lost all track of time. By the time he returned to his room, exhausted, the rain had let up somewhat and the room had become sultry and uncomfortable. He turned on the light and saw his unfinished dinner—it looked even more unappetizing than before. Since he did not feel like eating anything he decided to go on his rounds instead.

Parvathi Ammu was writing the case sheets but she stopped as soon as she saw Vasant. 'Doctor, I have the purse of that girl who met with the accident.'

'What will I do with it? Give it to the police.'

'I would have, except the constable has left. But there's a more pressing problem—I have to give instructions for her medication, and there is no one with the patient.'

'In that case, see if there are any phone numbers in her purse and call them up.'

'Doctor, I can't open her purse. If something goes missing I'll be blamed. Only you or the constable should do that.'

Parvathi Ammu took out the purse and put it on the table. Just then the constable walked in, looking guilty. 'Sorry, doctor, I had to go out, and got stuck in the traffic.'

'Doesn't matter now. Please open the purse and see if you can locate her contact details.'

The purse contained a small mirror, a comb, some tissues, a packet of bindis, a small bunch of keys, perfume and some money. It held no clue to her address, or any contact numbers. The constable looked irritated; tracing the girl's address in the pouring rain was not going to be an easy job. He guessed that the girl was not very wealthy and probably came from one of the city's many middle-class localities. 'Doctor, there is a small book in her purse, but I cannot understand the language.'

'*Bhasa Nataka Chakra*. It is a collection of Sanskrit plays,' Vasant said.

'Oh, you know this language?' The constable was glad, as he felt it might make his job easier. 'What is it?'

'It is Kannada, my mother tongue.'

He opened the first page and read the address of the owner. Anupama, No. 46, Pali Hill Road, Bandra.

Vasant told the nurse to inform the patient when she regained consciousness that her book was with him, and that he would see her again the next day.

Once he returned to his room, he started reading the book and, unbidden, his thoughts turned to his younger days. He remembered his father, Ramanna, and his deep voice. Ramanna had been a schoolteacher, and every evening after dinner, he would recite old Kannada poems

Sudha Murty

from *Jaimini Bharatha* while sitting in front of the Hanuman temple in the village. The cool breeze from the nearby pond would add to the serenity of the evening, and the villagers would listen to him with rapt attention. Vasant still remembered one of the poems:

There is no perfection in anything in life.
Even in the great river Ganga there are black serpents.
The beautiful Saraswathi has jet-black curls;
The moon has a dark spot
Because even in nature perfection is not possible.

He thought of Anupama for a fleeting moment before turning back to the book.

He was still reading the Kannada translation of *Bhasa Nataka Chakra*, when Satya walked in. His evening had obviously gone well for he was in very high spirits despite the lateness of the hour. He sat opposite Vasant and said, 'Hi, Boss! How was work? I hope you did not have too many difficult patients? Actually, come to think of it, Sunday is usually a lean day.'

'Yes, Satya, it wasn't all that difficult. I was lucky.' That was Vasant's standard response even on especially gruelling days.

'Why? Is there a special patient or some VIP?' Satya winked.

'Nothing like that. I found an interesting book. That is all.'

Satya was disappointed with Vasant's reply. 'What is so great about that? If you had asked me, I would have got some books for you. Is it the book that is interesting or the person who gave it to you?'

'Satya, I am not like you. Lady Luck doesn't even spare a glance at people like me!'

'Vasant, don't even say such things. You live like a hermit and that is why nothing exciting happens to you.

Listen to me. . .we have more than enough experience between the two of us. Let's resign from this job and start a clinic of our own in Andheri. With all the rich businessmen there, we'll be minting money in no time at all.'

Vasant did not want to comment on that. 'Satya, I think Vidya is calling you,' he said, looking out of the window.

Satya smiled and said, 'Don't try to change the subject. Anyway, I know you're not interested in private practice. Why on earth are you reading this? Today, there are enough DVDs in the market and people do not have time even to watch those. Umm. . .who else but you would want to read this Bhasa, hasa, chandrahasa. . .'

'Satya, please don't make fun of everything. If you knew anything about Sanskrit and its literature, you would enjoy reading this book, too.'

'Thank you for the suggestion. Vasant, try to understand that the language of love is also important. But you wouldn't understand it, and neither would you understand business!'

'Yes, Satya, you are right! I don't understand. I look at life in a more emotional way so I don't understand business. For me, emotions and sentiment are important. I don't care if those are at the cost of money.'

There was a knock at the door and Vidya entered. Satya dropped the discussion and left with her.

During his rounds the following evening, when Vasant approached Anupama's bed, he saw two girls sitting next to her, conversing softly.

On seeing Vasant, Anupama became silent. Though Vasant was not talkative by nature, he asked Anupama, 'How are you feeling now?'

Anupama replied to him in Kannada, 'I am fine, thank you, doctor.'

'How do you know that I speak Kannada?' asked Vasant.

'The duty nurse told me that you had taken my book; I knew then.' Anupama realized that she was speaking Kannada after a long time.

'I haven't finished reading your book yet. It takes a while to read such literature.'

'Please keep it for as long as you want. It is my book.'

Vasant now turned his attention to her leg. 'How is the pain now?'

'My leg hurts a lot.'

'Yes, that is because you have a fracture. It will be all right once the plaster is in place. I will prescribe some tablets that I want you to take regularly for the pain.' Vasant wrote out the prescription and left.

Later that night, Vasant continued reading the book, and pondered over the notes written in the margins. They showed a depth of knowledge that surprised him. Another thing that puzzled him was the fact that although several young girls visited her during the day, Anupama was alone all night long. He could not bring himself to ask her anything about it as it was against his nature to pry.

The next day, Anupama asked him anxiously, 'Doctor, how long do I have to stay in the hospital?'

'At least for a few more days. I will discharge you after assessing your progress.' Anupama's face fell.

'How is it that your sisters have not come today?' he asked, attempting to distract her.

'They are not my sisters. I am a professor in a college. Some of them are my colleagues, and some my students.'

'Are you from Bombay?' Vasant was examining her leg.

'Yes.'

'What about your family?'

Vasant caught the expression of pain and grief that flitted across her face.

'I don't have any.'

Vasant stopped examining her. He asked most of his patients such random questions, more to divert their attention than because he wished to know more about them. But, today he felt that his questions had distressed Anupama.

'I'm sorry if I have hurt you.'

'No, doctor, I have learnt to accept reality.'

Satya could not help noticing that among his patients, Vasant was most comfortable talking to Anupama, and he also spent more time with her.

'How is your special patient today?' he teased Vasant later.

'I don't know what you're talking about,' Vasant replied shortly.

'I'm asking about the patient who gave you the Kannada book.'

'Satya, don't make fun of her. If she hears this, she might feel uncomfortable. She has already had enough pain in her life. People who have leukoderma feel like outcasts in our society because we look down upon them. Though it is only what is called a "cosmetic" disease, our society has not yet accepted that.'

'Sorry, Vasant, I did not mean to sound callous. She is stunningly beautiful; but a few white patches have spoiled her beauty, like a drop of lemon in milk.'

'I really don't understand why people look down upon such patients. I worked for a year in the Dermatology Department. People with leukoderma suffer from a deficiency in the pigmentation of their skin, that's all. They are otherwise perfectly normal. No one has proved that it is hereditary; it is certainly not contagious, and often with proper treatment people have been completely cured. I have seen it happen myself.'

'Come on, Vasant, I only said what others usually feel. Normally, such people are shunned in the marriage market. Even if one of the parents has leukoderma, the groom or bride will think twice before considering such an alliance. You are an idealist. Would you marry such a girl?'

By then, Vidya had arrived at the other end of the ward, and Satya hurried towards her.

Vasant mulled over Satya's comment and then dismissed it. *My marriage! Let me cross that bridge when I come to it!*

❧

Anupama was able to walk now, and she was going to be discharged the next day. She had been a good patient, and had followed the doctor's advice sincerely, so her progress had been fast. Every day, she would slowly walk from her room to Vasant's chambers and then go back, as she had been told to practise walking a little.

When she was leaving the hospital, Vasant told her, 'You are fine now. Make sure you eat well and you will recover fast.'

She paid her bill and thanked Vasant, 'Thank you, doctor, for all that you have done for me. I cannot adequately express my gratitude for all that you have done. Being able to speak Kannada again made me feel so much at home.'

Vasant felt a little embarrassed as he was not used to being thanked so profusely. He said, 'If you really want to thank me, invite me to see the play that you are directing.'

Anupama was surprised, 'How do you know about that?'

'Satya told me. It seems one of the plays that you directed received an award. It was announced in the Kannada Sangha at Matunga. We go there often.'

'By all means. Actually I am directing a play for the Dusshera festival. Please do come. I will send the invitation.'

'Two of us will come, but please don't send passes. I want to buy tickets. No performing art should be seen free of cost.'

'Entry is free, so don't worry about tickets. Do bring your wife.'

Vasant laughed heartily. 'I'm still unmarried. I don't have anyone either, like you. I will come with Satya. He's my roommate.'

Anupama felt a little awkward and said, 'I am sorry, doctor.'

'Why are you apologizing? You never asked me anything. I chose to tell you about myself.'

Anupama had also become well acquainted with Satya by this time. She said goodbye, gave him her visiting card and left, saying, 'Keep in touch.'

~

A few months later, Satya and Vasant went to attend their colleague's wedding in Bandra. They were both surprised when they saw Anupama there. She had recovered completely and looked happy.

'Hello doctor, it's so nice to meet you again,' Anupama smiled.

Satya happily started a conversation with her. 'It is not always nice to meet doctors! They remind one of sickness and surgery.'

Anupama disagreed, 'No, doctors always remind me of service and hope!'

Vasant interrupted, 'How come you are here?'

'The bride is my student.'

'The groom is our colleague,' Satya told her.

There was a two-hour break between the wedding ceremony and lunch.

'My house is close by. I must go and check on something. Please come and have a cup of tea before lunch,' insisted Anupama.

Vasant was keen on getting to know her better and immediately agreed.

'Not now. We will come some other time,' said Satya who was in no mood to exert himself.

'Why don't you go ahead? We'll come in half an hour.' It was Vasant who took the lead although it was unusual for him.

'How will you find my house? I could go later if you want.'

'Don't worry, Satya Prakash is here. We will find our way.' Satya was surprised by Vasant's eagerness, although he knew what was going on. Once Anupama left, he asked with a mischievous smile, 'Vasant, why are we going to a former patient's house?'

'Instead of sitting here and wasting time, we might as well go. Besides, she is a good person. My mother always told me that one should make an effort to meet people when one doesn't need something from them. Only then will relationships develop.'

Satya made a show of reluctance before following Vasant out of the marriage hall.

'When I make a lot of money I would like to buy a house in Pali Hill. That is one of my missions in life. Look at all the rich and famous people who live here; they're either film stars or business magnates. Unlike most parts of Bombay, it still has some bungalows and trees left. What about you, Vasant? You never talk about your future.'

'What about my future? You know appa died of rabies after being bitten by a dog in the village where we lived. That incident upsets me even now. If only there had been a good clinic and a doctor in the village, appa would have lived.

I want to get some experience here, then go back and start my own clinic in the village. Money has never held any attraction for me. I will get more satisfaction by saving people like appa, rather than by staying in Bombay and making a lot of money.'

'Vasant, don't you require a lot of capital to realize this dream?'

'Not really. I have my own house, which I will convert into a clinic. I have saved some money and I also own some land. I'll manage. It will be a simple life with not much money.'

'What about medicines and nursing?'

'I will charge the rich, and with that money I'll buy medicines for the poor.'

'What about marriage? Does that feature in your plans? What if your wife says no to such a life after you get married?'

'I am aware of the risk, Satya. That is why I am still unmarried. I will marry only when I find the woman who will agree to support my plans.'

By then they had reached Anupama's house.

It was an old, whitewashed bungalow, with a beautiful, neat garden. There were coconut trees, guava and mango trees, and flower-beds in front of the house, with a cross in the corner. The name of the house was written on the gatepost: Mary Villa.

Anupama was waiting for them.

The interior of the house, which reflected the taste of the occupant, was as simple as the outside. Fresh cut flowers in a vase adorned the centre table.

'This is one of the most beautiful houses I have ever seen,' Satya remarked.

'This is my friend's house. She moved to Australia after her marriage and asked me to stay on, telling me to take care of the house and not to bother with the rent. The house is divided into two portions. I stay in one portion and the other is locked. Dolly's mother comes here once in a while and stays there.'

'How long can you stay here?'

'As long as we have mutual love, affection and trust. I cannot measure that.'

'What happens if you refuse to vacate the place?'

'Why should I keep something that is not mine? If we keep things that don't belong to us, we are worse than beggars. Breach of trust and failure to honour one's commitments are the worst sins that I can think of.'

Anupama realized that, subconsciously, she had been thinking of Anand and his betrayal, and that her words sounded unnaturally harsh.

Vasant was busy examining her library while Satya and she talked. 'Anupama, you have a rare collection of books. I have heard about Ashwagosha who wrote the famous *Buddha Charitha Manasa*. People say that it was the first drama in Indian literature.'

'Yes, doctor. There might have been many other dramatists, but we do not have any of their works. What fascinates me about Ashwagosha is that he is a person who identifies with his mother, unlike others who identify with their fathers.'

'Satya, are you getting bored?' Vasant asked.

'Even though it is Greek and Latin to me, I am enjoying it.'

'Doctor,' Anupama said to Vasant, 'Sanskrit is my subject, so I know it fairly well. How are you so well versed in it? It is so unusual to meet someone outside the classroom who is fond of the language.'

'There is a reason for that. My father was a Sanskrit teacher in our village. When I was a child I learnt it by listening to my father's recitation from the classics. I have never had any formal instruction in the language. My love for Sanskrit is linked with memories of my parents. Today, they are both gone, but I still continue to read the Sanskrit classics.'

All too soon it was time for them to return to the wedding celebrations. As they were stepping out, Anupama said, 'If you need to borrow any books, any time, please let me know. That is the one thing I can offer.'

❧

Monday was Out-Patients' Day, and everyone in the hospital was busy. As in all government hospitals, it was proving to be very difficult to control the OPD crowd.

Vasant was intent on going to his department when suddenly he heard someone call out to him, 'Hi, Vasant!'

He turned to see Seema waving to him. He was surprised; Seema was supposed to be in America.

'Hello, Seema,' he waved back.

'How are you, Vasant?'

'I am fine, how are you?'

'How do I look?' Seema asked, smiling.

Vasant looked at her. She had become fairer and had put on some weight. Glamorous Seema was looking even more fashionable now! Her stylishly trimmed hair, perfectly manicured nails, and transparent chiffon sari enhanced her sophistication.

'I am surprised to see you here,' Vasant commented.

'My sister is getting married and papa insisted that I must be here at least for a month. So here I am.' She opened her bag and pulled out a wedding invitation.

Sudha Murty

'What about your family?' Vasant asked as he took the invitation from her.

'Oh! My baby is not well—he's six months old, and in spite of all our efforts, he's been bitten by mosquitoes. My husband is looking after him. Vasant, don't miss the wedding. You must come.'

'If I am not on duty that day, I'll definitely come. Where is the wedding?'

'At the Taj. My sister's in-laws are very rich and they insisted that the wedding had to be very grand. Even if you are on duty, please get out of it and come.'

'I'll try.'

'Vasant, you haven't changed a bit. You're meeting a friend after three years. Won't you even invite me home for tea?'

'Sorry, Seema, I don't have a home. If you want, I can take you to Lakshmi Bhavan, our favourite college-time haunt.'

Seema was horrified. 'Come on Vasant, how can I eat there now? It is so dirty, and there are all sorts of infections floating around in Bombay!'

'But you used to love eating there.'

'It was different then.'

'All right. I'll take you to a good restaurant then.'

'I am very busy with shopping and wedding preparations now. I'll tell you when I'm free and you can take me then.'

'Do you like living and working in the US?'

'Oh Vasant, I make so much money there. Together, my husband and I are minting money. If a bright person like you were there, you could have earned so much. You are wasting your time in India.'

'I don't think so, Seema. You have not seen the real world here; it needs people like us. As in so many other matters, let's agree to disagree.'

Seema laughed as they made their way to Vasant's department. 'By the way, when are you getting married?'

'I have not found the right girl yet.'

Seema and Vasant had been classmates in college. Seema was an ambitious girl who had always had a soft corner for Vasant. Once, she had even expressed her desire to marry Vasant, but on condition that he settle in America. When she had perceived his true bent of mind, she had changed her mind quickly, married someone in the US, and settled there. Vasant had never mentioned this to anybody. He felt that Seema had made the right decision.

They stopped outside his department. 'Vasant, when will I see you again?'

'When I come to your sister's wedding.'

She was not sure that he would come and, sensing her thoughts, Vasant said, 'If I could come to your wedding, I can come to your sister's wedding as well. Can I go now? My patients are waiting.'

Seema smiled and waved goodbye before heading off.

❧

When Vasant returned to his room after finishing with his OPD patients, he was surprised to see Satya lying on the bed. Normally, he would not have been in the room at that time. When he looked at him keenly, he was surprised to see that Satya's eyes were red and his face swollen. When he touched his forehead, it was burning hot.

'Satya, what happened? You have fever!'

Instead of replying, Satya started crying.

'Satya, is there any bad news from home? How are your parents?'

Still, Satya did not reply. His eyes were focused on the table. On it was a beautiful wedding invitation with letters etched in gold on a red velvet background that seemed to exude affluence. It was Vidya's wedding card.

Vasant was surprised. He had always thought that Vidya and Satya would get married. Now he could understand why Satya was in the state he was in. Nothing Vasant said would bring Satya any consolation.

'When did this happen?' Vasant asked gently.

'Today. She invited everybody, including me.'

'Satya, do you think she is getting married under family pressure?'

'No. I don't think so. The boy is a doctor. His parents are also doctors in the US. A good catch. And nobody can force Vidya to do anything, let alone get married.'

'But how could she do this to you?'

'Vasant, I've been impractical and emotional. Vidya is definitely more calculating. She has thought things over. What assets do I have—a small house in Mysore, the responsibility of getting my three sisters married and of educating my brother?'

'Did you discuss all this with Vidya?

'Yes. She'd said it wouldn't be a problem. But then, she met this boy who is far more eligible. I suppose she was just biding her time till she found the right match.'

'Satya, there is no point in brooding over this. It is good that it ended when it did; far better now than being hurt after marriage.'

For the next few days, Satya hardly ate anything. He was depressed and did not talk much. One day he began vomiting, and when this continued for a while, Satya grew worried. A blood test confirmed that he was suffering from jaundice.

The diagnosis further lowered his spirits. Though it was not a critical disease, the patient would require good food, care, and rest. Satya did not want to go to Mysore, but he did not have any close friends or relatives in Bombay either with whom he could stay. The hotel food that he had been eating all along was definitely out of the question.

Vasant came up with a suggestion. 'Why don't we ask someone who can cook to send you a dabba so that you can have home-cooked food while you're recovering?' By this time, Vasant had begun to attend Anupama's plays regularly, at different locations in Bombay; and he also visited her library quite often. Their casual acquaintance had now turned into a deep friendship. He had no doubt that she would be able to help him now. After all, she had a large network of students and friends.

'Satya, I have an idea. I'll ask Anupama to look for someone who can cook a "diet" meal and send it here. We will pay for it. I'm sure Anupama will be able to help us.'

Without waiting for Satya's reply he immediately called up Anupama.

After hearing him out, Anupama replied, 'Vasant, I have another suggestion. My maid, Sakkubai, stays with me; she is a good lady. If Satya doesn't have any objections, he can come and stay in our front room. I can cook a suitable meal for him, and Sakkubai will look after him day and night. Of course, I won't insist on this. If you still want the food to be sent across to your room, I will make enquiries and find out someone who can supply the food.'

Vasant had never expected such a generous offer and said, 'I will get back to you after speaking to Satya.'

Satya was hesitant about accepting the offer. 'Vasant, I don't know her as well as you do. How can I impose on her like this? I can pay Sakkubai, but what about Anupama? I feel very awkward about accepting this offer.'

Satya, the extrovert, had become more serious now. The shock of Vidya's defection had changed his outlook.

'Come on Satya. She is our friend and, as far as I can see, this is the best option. You won't be staying there forever, and we can always return the favour in some form to Anupama. As far as I know, she is not the sort of person who expects anything in return.'

Satya agreed to move from Bombay Central to Anupama's Bandra house. She had kept the room clean and tidy. She had spread a printed sheet on the bed and placed a vase with some fresh flowers in a corner. There was a world of difference between Satya's room and this one!

Anupama looked after Satya as if he were a part of her family. Once, his temperature went up very high and she stayed awake by his side the whole night. Another day, Satya vomited all over Anupama, before she could help him to the basin. The stench filled the room and Satya felt extremely embarrassed. But Anupama showed no sign of being disgusted or upset. She cleaned the floor and came back freshened after a bath.

When Satya apologized for what had happened, she said, 'Satya, don't feel sorry. A patient is like a child. . . dependent on someone. When I broke my leg, you, Vasant and the nurses did everthing possible for my recovery. I am not doing anything different.'

Satya was supposed to stay for a week but he postponed his departure. During his stay there, Satya had been observing Anupama. He had always thought of her as a beautiful but unfortunate woman; and he had pitied her. But now he felt differently. He saw that she was invariably cheerful, and always ready to help; she did not seem the least bit bothered about the white patches on her body that spoiled her beauty.

Satya began comparing Anupama and Vidya, subconsciously. For Vidya, material comforts and beauty were very important. Helping others was something she would consider a waste of time. She had always been self-centred. *Was Vidya devoid of the softer sentiments,* he wondered again and again. How could she change her mind so casually, as if she were changing a dress, and marry someone else, whereas he had been ready to face all opposition from home to marry her?

Anupama was aware that Satya had become quieter and more sober because his relationship had ended abruptly. So she spent time talking to him about all sorts of things, to take his mind off his broken affair.

'Satya, in spite of being a doctor, why are you so worried about a common illness such as this?'

'Anupama, sometimes, ignorance is bliss. But we, as doctors, know so much about disease and sickness that we cannot help feeling apprehensive occasionally. My sisters in Mysore will not understand all the implications or worry about them as much as I do. You know, Anupama, whenever I look at you, I think of my sister Sandhya—she would have cared for me like this.'

'Satya, I have helped you the way any human being would help another; nothing more and nothing less. I don't like being caught in relationships of convenience. I don't want to be anyone's 'sister' or 'aunt'. When two men can be friends and two women can be friends, surely a man and a woman can also be just friends.'

Satya was taken aback by her blunt answer. It was very uncharacteristic of her. He looked at her and realized that someone had deeply hurt her at some time in her life.

✦

It was Satya's last day at Anupama's house. After that, he would go back to his untidy room and eat the oily food served at Lakshmi Bhavan. He could see the Bandra seashore from his window, as he thought about Anupama. He knew nothing about her—whether she was married or unmarried, or whether she had any relatives. During the two weeks he had been in her house, only her students and friends had visited her. He knew she was from Karnataka, nothing more. Sometimes he thought about talking to her of her past, but he had never been able to bring himself to do so.

Anupama came and sat beside him. She looked at Satya and said, 'Forget the past, Satya, think about the future. Start a new life. '

Satya smiled unhappily and said, 'Anupama, you and Vasant do not know what it is to fall in love and then lose the person you love. Love is a precious emotion and when it is wasted on the wrong person, you tend to become emotionally reticent. Only people who are very fortunate fall in love with and marry the same person.'

Anupama did not reply. After some time she said, 'You're wrong about me, Satya. I know what it is to lose in love. I was once in love with someone. We got married, but later, my husband abandoned me.'

Satya was taken aback.

Anupama continued. 'When I was in college, I acted in a play called *Mahashweta*. Anand saw me on stage and fell in love with me. Despite the differences in our status, we got married. I am from a poor family and my mother-in-law was indifferent to me from the beginning. A few months after our wedding, Anand went abroad for further studies, and I was about to join him when I developed a white patch on my foot. My mother-in-law's indifference changed to cruelty as she accused me of having had this affliction before marriage. She said I had deceived Anand

and tricked him into marrying me, and cast me out of the house. I wrote several letters to my husband but he never replied. He had loved Mahashweta as a heroine. But when in real life I developed this white patch, and became a real Mahashweta, the White One, he couldn't handle it. This Mahashweta was not acceptable to him. Just as you throw away old clothes and buy new ones, my in-laws got him remarried. Up to this day, nobody has bothered about me. Your life is definitely better than mine. You must thank your stars that you have only failed in love, not in marriage. Marriage is a lifelong commitment, and I know only too well the pain it causes when someone fails to honour that commitment.'

Satya felt as if he had been listening to a story. But, unfortunately, the white patch on Anupama's hand belied the feeling.

Anupama continued. 'Anand has a sister. Girija had a clandestine affair that only I knew about. But today, she is married to a person of wealth and status. Who says life is fair? It is better to understand the vicissitudes of life and solve our own problems in the manner we find appropriate. I have learnt that repeated success makes a person arrogant, while occasional failure makes an individual more mature.'

'Anupama, who taught you all this philosophy?' Satya asked.

'My experiences have taught me this. I have come to realize that courage and confidence are the real wealth in life. Education can improve your chances of success, but ultimately you have to face life all alone. I don't depend on any guru nor do I read any philosophy. My conscience is my guru and it guides me well.'

Satya picked up courage and asked, 'Anupama, I will ask you a personal question. If you do not want to answer,

I will not mind. But I am curious—do you think of Anand often?'

'I do sometimes, but I want to forget him. It is better to concentrate on things that give me confidence and happiness. I like history, literature and drama. I am extremely fond of my students as they are of me. I believe that when students love the teacher, they learn to love the subject, too. A teacher is forever young at heart. History has taught me a great lesson. People who built forts and won many kingdoms are not remembered today. I don't do my work so that somebody should remember me; I do it because it gives me satisfaction and contentment.'

'Anupama, do you consider yourself unfortunate?'

'No, Satya. Of the thousands of flowers that blossom on a tree only a few will bear fruit. And out of those few fruits, insects and squirrels will eat some. The tree does not keep anything for itself. Does that mean that the life of the tree is wasted? I have great friends and good students, and I am economically independent. I neither worry about the past, nor brood over the future. I accept life as it comes and I don't have any regrets.'

The morning breeze was pleasant but there was a nip in the air. Anand wrapped a scarf around his neck, afraid that the weather would give him a cold, and then a cough.

In life, every decision has a side-effect, too, he mused, *and we should always calculate the pros and cons of a particular course of action before taking a decision. But somehow.* . .Anand sighed. His mind stubbornly continued to recall the things he wished to forget, made a conscious effort to forget. He tried to rationalize his decisions, but his mind was in constant turmoil.

Normally, he took his morning walk in his garden, which was spread over an acre of land. There were so many fruit trees and flower-beds that the combined fragrance would waft in the breeze and make the entire house smell sweet. When Girija came from Bangalore with her baby daughter for a visit, the gardener plucked the flowers from various plants and strung them for her to wear in her hair. Radhakka was no longer interested in all those things; she had grown old, and arthritis had crippled her body.

And what of Anupama? Anand's thoughts stopped as he reached the parijata tree. The ground below it was covered with its beautiful and delicate flowers. Radhakka always said, 'This is the flower brought by Lord Krishna to please his queen, Rukmini.' As far as Anand was concerned, the parijata always reminded him of Anupama.

When he had left for England, his heart had been in India. Anand was very ambitious by nature. In an attempt to discourage him from going, Anupama had said, 'We just got married. Why do you have to go to England now? We already have everything we could possibly need. Besides, Mother is growing old; we should stay near her.' Anand had told her, 'Anu, you don't understand life. If you go to England and get a degree, then the people here respect you. And, after all, it is just for three years.' His mother's wishes and his wife's entreaties had not dissuaded him in the least.

In England, Anand had met Nalini Pathak. She was a doctor from Bombay, who believed that, with her fair skin, green eyes, and auburn hair, she was very beautiful. Anand, however, thought she was not a patch on Anupama. Nalini was hurt when he made no attempts to be friendly with her. She had approached him one evening and said, 'Anand, don't you have any time at all to talk to your colleagues?'

'No, I hardly get any free time.'

'This is the best period of our lives. We are young and we don't have any responsibilities; we should enjoy ourselves now.'

'That is true, Nalini. But this is also the time for us to study and build our careers.' Anand cut her short and went away.

He was eagerly waiting for Anupama to arrive. Then, Nalini would understand the meaning of real beauty. He would feel happy for days after speaking to Anupama or receiving a letter from her. He could have brought her with him, but his mother had put her foot down. 'Anand, I have accepted the girl you have chosen, and she should accept my condition. She can go only after the Lakshmi puja is completed successfully. Don't hurt me by saying no.'

Anand could not refuse his mother's plea. She had not only consented to the alliance without a fuss but had also borne the expenditure of the entire wedding. Had it not been for her, he would never have been able to marry his dream girl. It was a question of two months. He would bide his time and somehow get through the separation. Anand had no way of anticipating the tornado that would sweep through his life.

It had begun with the fateful letter he received from Radhakka. Though it contained only a few lines, it broke his heart.

Your wife Anupama has a white patch on her foot, which she had concealed from everyone. It seems she has been taking treatment secretly from before the marriage. Girija had also suspected it. Now she has gone to her father's place. I have spoken to the doctor and he says it might take a long time to cure her. She must complete the treatment before coming back. The presence of a woman with a white patch is not acceptable during auspicious occasions such as Lakshmi puja; I will not risk the purity of the household. That is my faith and belief.

Anand was aghast. He read the letter several times, unable to imagine Anupama disfigured with white patches. Anupama's letter reached him the next day. He opened it reluctantly—it contained her version of the story.

Anand had always had a weakness for beauty. It inspired him to always choose the best of everything. The financial status of his family had only served to encourage his predilection. His friends had often joked, 'Hey Anand, considering you take so long to choose your clothes, how will you find someone to marry? You will probably be old by the time you get married. We may not have the opportunity to see your bride at all.'

But Anand had married before any of his friends, and his bride had been the most beautiful girl in the neighbourhood. His friends had even been a bit jealous of his good fortune. 'Congratulations, Anand. She fulfils all your criteria,' they had said. Anand had felt then that he was the luckiest man on earth. Anupama was not just his wife, she was the index of his pride.

When Anand had first found out that she had leukoderma, he was filled with revulsion. As a doctor he knew that it was not always curable. If it did not respond to treatment, it would spread to her face, to her red lips, her beautiful fingers. . .everywhere. He did not wish to imagine how she would look. There was nothing he could do, and the more he thought about her, the uglier she became in his imagination. What would his friends say? 'Oh! Look at poor Anand. He takes so much time to choose a simple shirt, and if the shirt starts to fade, he discards it. What will he do with his wife?' Some would say, 'Serves him right for being such a perfectionist.'

Anand had never experienced failure in his life till then. Life had always been a bed of roses for him. Some people thought it was luck, but his mother belived that it was the result of her prayers. Facing disappointment for the first time in his life, he found that he was unable to cope with it. Unlike his mother, Anand knew for sure that there had been no white patch on Anupama's foot before their marriage. *I wish Anupama had had this condition before we got married. Things would have been so different then.*

He met Nalini Pathak on his way back from college a few days later. She said, 'Oh Anand, have you already started preparing for the exams?'

Anand did not reply. He was lost in thought about life's exams, which were far more difficult. *Once you fail, it is the end. This is the only life we have—who knows for sure if one is reborn? We can enjoy or destroy our life. Everything is in our own hands*, mused Anand. He had to make a decision. Anupama had begged him to let her join him in England to escape malicious talk back home. But if she joined him here, there would be others who would talk.

Nalini Pathak would say, 'Anand, I am so sorry about Anupama. I think she should go to a good dermatologist.' Every imagined word was hurtful.

Anupama's letter had come some weeks ago, but Anand had not replied to it. Anand began to rationalize. *Anupama is being treated by the best doctor. I shall wait and see what happens. There is no way I can call avva and ask her to take Anupama back. She is old-fashioned, and once she makes up her mind, she won't change. And in such a situation it is better that Anupama is with her parents rather than avva. I'm sure Anupama will overcome any hurdles she faces. Did she not sell a thousand-rupee ticket to a stranger like me? And did she not have the courage to stand in front of thousands of people and enact scenes of sorrow, of passion without feeling awkward? It's best if she handles the present situation on her own. I shall write to her after some time, once everyone has calmed down. She will also feel better about it.*

In the meantime, he received a letter from her father, begging for his daughter's happiness. Anand thought about his unborn children. Though it had not been proved that the disease was hereditary, he couldn't take the risk. If his children were also affected, then his state would be the same as Shamanna's. Anand shivered at the thought of that humiliation. Even in the cold English winter, he started sweating. The only way to get out of the mess was to divert his attention.

Anand immersed himself in work, taking on extra duties in the hospital. He forgot that there was a helpless young girl waiting for his decision, somewhere in a village thousands of miles away.

✧

Sudha Murty

Anand continued to receive letters from his mother. While they dwelt on her own health and conveyed news of the family, there was never any mention of Anupama. He began to write to his mother less frequently, but would call her up once in a while. India had become synonymous with bad memories for him. Anupama's letters arrived—full of tears, difficulties, and information about the progress of the disease. After a while they stopped coming.

Then Girija's marriage was fixed. Anand flew down days before the wedding like a guest. His mother made it a point to introduce him informally to many people, and he soon became aware of her intentions.

His mother broached the topic once Girija had left for her in-laws' place. 'Anand, I am worried about you. Now that Girija has married well, I want you to settle down, too.'

Anand did not answer.

'Last time, some strangers whose background we didn't know used beauty to trap you. This time you should marry into a known family.'

Anand still kept quiet.

'Anupama has not tried to contact us even once since she left home. Perhaps she doesn't want to stay with you. I heard she wants a divorce and alimony. Poor girl! Let us be fair and pay her something. Though she deceived us, I'm willing to overlook that. But I don't want you to wait indefinitely.'

Irritated, Anand rose from his seat. Radhakka continued. 'Do you want to become an ascetic? Our family should grow and our lineage should continue. We have so much property. I want my grandchildren to inherit it.'

Anand felt her words pierce through him, but he did not know what to say. Radhakka had tears in her eyes on the day he left, 'Anand, when will I see you again?'

'Very soon.'

'Shall I go ahead and find a girl for you?'

'Let me think about it.'

Though Anand left without giving a firm answer, Radhakka assumed it was a yes.

Anand completed his degree successfully and continued to practise in England for a while. One day, a couple came to his hospital. The wife was using crutches and the husband was helping her. There was also a baby in his arms. He explained, 'My wife lost her legs in a car accident. Now she is unwell, and the baby is irritable. That is why we are here.'

As Anand quietly examined the wife, the husband kept talking. 'We are God-fearing people. That is why we make Him the witness in everything. In my marriage vows I had sworn that we would be together until death. It is my duty to help her whenever she is in difficulty.'

Anand was touched by his words. Even in the West, where divorce was easy, this man had chosen to take care of his crippled wife because of his commitment to the marriage vows he had made. Anand thought of Anupama. He, too, had made many promises in front of Agni and all the guests who had come to bless them during the wedding ceremony. Now they were parted, but not by death. Had he done the right thing? His mother kept insisting that he should remarry. He would have to make similar promises to another woman. What was the guarantee that this marriage would last? Having lived alone for so long, he would find it difficult to adjust to someone else's ways. He had not found happiness after marrying a girl of his own choice; would he be happy in a marriage arranged by his mother?

❧

Anand returned to India some months later to set up a practice in his home town. In the sprawling expanse of

Sudha Murty

Lakshmi Nivas, there were only three people now—Anand, Radhakka, who had fallen down and broken her hip, and her helper, Narayanachar.

When Radhakka realized that Anand was not willing to remarry, she was very upset. She cried and fasted for a few days, but stopped when nothing came out of it. So, she reconciled herself to the situation by saying, 'I cannot change his fate. Whatever will be, will be.' But, deep inside, she remained very upset. The only change in the house came when Girija visited with her daughter.

Anand could not find any peace in his home. He was constantly reminded of a past that he wished to forget. Though there was not a trace of Anupama or of any of her belongings in the house, the very fact that she had lived there for two months was a source of irritation and distress to Anand. He decided to move into Girija's room on the ground floor.

He was arranging his books in the chest of drawers, which had been purchased by his father in Bangalore. It was made of rosewood and exquisitely crafted. A few books fell from his hand when he was putting them in the drawer. When he bent down to pick them up, he noticed a small drawer at the back, which was not visible from the front. Curious, he pulled it open, and found a letter and sundry bits of paper in it.

Why was the letter kept there? Was it an important letter, or did it hold secrets? Anand started reading it.

My darling Girija,

Last night when you were going from my room, I think your sister-in-law, Anupama, saw you. She may be aware of our relationship. I will always cherish the time I spent with you in Belur-Halebeedu. I get so much joy when you are with me. At times I feel we should live like this forever. But I am aware of my situation; and I know that being born in a rich family you are used to a certain lifestyle, and want to marry a rich man. I agree with you—as long as we are here, we should spend our days happily. Afterwards, we may not meet each other at all. We will probably be strangers to one another. Will you come tonight at 8 p.m.?

Lovingly yours,

Vijay.

Anand was stunned.

Girija was not a starry-eyed teenager who had been coerced by someone. She had been a willing participant in a clandestine relationship just for fun, before her marriage! His own sister—he couldn't believe it. Even he had never looked at another woman after he had left Anupama, though there had been no dearth of opportunities.

None of the other women who had been born in the house, and even those who had married into the family, had ever behaved like this. He thought of Girija. What guarantee was there that she and her boyfriend were not meeting even after marriage? Even though he knew it would come as a shock to Radhakka, he thought it would be best to tell her about the affair. He hoped Girija would heed their mother's advice instead of dismissing it, like she did his.

At dinner, when Radhakka saw Anand's worried face and a letter in his hand, she asked, 'Whose letter is that?'

'It is Girija's. From someone called Vijay.'

Radhakka's face reflected her unhappiness. 'Why should we talk about it now? Let us forget the past.'

'No, avva. I want to know what happened,' Anand was adamant.

Radhakka sighed deeply, 'Don't you remember Vijay who was staying in our outhouse for a while? He was Girija's classmate. He was good at his studies, but from a very poor family. His father was a cook. Vijay would do little odd jobs for us. Girija was friendly with him.'

'Is that all? There must be much more than that.'

'Yes. When I came to know, I sent Vijay away and started looking out for a boy for Girija. Today she is happily married.'

'If Girija and Vijay loved each other, you should have got them married. Even Anupama was from a poor family but you allowed me to marry her.'

'That was different. Anand, you must learn to be practical in life. You can bring a daughter-in-law from a poor family into your house; but never send your daughter to a poor family. How could I have married off a princess like Girija to a beggar like Vijay? Or told people that my daughter's father-in-law is a cook? What would they have said? Think of our status in society!'

'But Girija loved him.'

'No, Girija did not love him. When I told her that I was going to look for a bridegroom for her she was very happy.'

Anand was unable to understand the workings of his mother's mind. He had always assumed that his mother was an orthodox woman, but quite guileless. For the first time, he realized that his impression of her was wrong, that she was pragmatic and opportunistic.

'Anand, who told you about this? Was it Anupama?'

'Why are you talking about her?'

'Because only she knew about it, apart from me.'

Suddenly, Anupama appeared to him in a different light. His doubts and misgivings about the way he had treated her came surging back. Yes, Anupama had contracted an affliction that marred her external beauty, but she was still pure at heart. She had been shunned and abandoned only because of one white patch. On the other hand, Girija, who had had a sordid affair before her marriage, was held in high esteem in society and at home.

Anand felt responsible for Anupama's misfortunes. Why had he allowed his sense of fairness and his judgment to become so warped that he had turned away when she had needed him the most? Why had he shirked from honouring the vows he had taken when he had married her? Why had he assumed, all these years, that his mother was right? A deep sense of guilt and shame pervaded his mind.

Whatever I have done was wrong, but the time that I have lost cannot be recovered. However, I must rectify the mistakes I have made and shape the future properly. I will beg Anupama to forgive me. She is far superior to anyone I know—in morals, intellect and conduct. With new-found determination he got up.

Looking at his face, Radhakka asked him, 'Where are you going?'

'I am going to bring Anupama back into my life again. I just hope it is not too late.'

❧

It was Deepavali, the festival of lights. All of Bombay seemed to be exchanging gifts, consuming enormous quantities of sweets, and throwing parties.

Satya had left for Mysore where his mother and sisters were eagerly waiting for him. Anupama had helped him buy gifts for his family. When he had tried to buy her a sari as a gift, she had refused to accept it.

'Satya, I have everything I want in life, and I am very thankful for that. When I need something I will definitely ask you.'

Vasant had tactfully intervened, 'Satya, buy lots of crackers for Anupama and I will help her burn them on Deepavali night.'

Since Vasant did not have a family with whom he could celebrate the festival, Anupama invited him home.

'Vasant, please stay for dinner. I have called my students, too.'

Vasant happily accepted her invitation. It had been a long time since he had celebrated Deepavali. How different it had been in his childhood! Even though they had been poor, they had celebrated the festival with great enthusiasm and in keeping with its true spirit. His mother would give him a leisurely oil-bath early in the morning, despite his protests. And then she would prepare sweets for the festival. Although they had lacked the comforts that money could buy, their poverty had cast no shadow on their happiness.

Vasant arrived early at Mary Villa on Deepavali. He had bought a collection of Bernard Shaw's plays as a gift for Anupama. She looked relaxed and cheerful, as usual. Watching her, he wondered if she had ever felt any unhappiness. Her face always glowed with contentment— it was as if she was one of the lucky few who were happy all the time.

'You shouldn't have bought me a gift, Vasant.'

'My mother taught me never to go empty-handed to meet a friend.'

Anupama's mind suddenly went back to her mother. She did not have a single photograph of her. If she had lived, she would probably have given her advice just as Vasant's mother had.

Vasant was looking at the beautiful rajanigandha, marigold and cosmos blooming in her garden. They were all dancing in the evening breeze in harmony with one another; and yet, they were all so different. He looked at Anupama and, noticing her silence, said, 'It is difficult to forget one's mother, isn't it?'

Sadly, Anupama answered, 'I never had the luxury of knowing my mother. It is impossible to replace a mother's love.'

With her father, it had always been more a bond of duty than love. When she had got a job in Bombay, she had sent half her salary to her father. But she had never felt like going back home. She never shared her difficulties with him either. Her father had mixed feelings about her. He was happy that Anupama was economically independent and had settled down. But he was an old-fashioned person; and he felt that she should go back to her husband. He believed that a woman's ultimate sanctuary should be her in-laws' house—single women were not respected in society. Shamanna was worried that people would gossip about her and it would reflect on him. He repeatedly wrote to her to plead with Anand to take her back, and not get upset with him. Anupama found such advice distasteful after the emotional trauma she had endured. Despite that, she knew that Shamanna cared deeply for her.

One day, a telegram came from the village—Shamanna had died of a heart attack. With his death, the last link with her past had been severed. Sometimes, she felt that perhaps her problems and the way she lived now had caused him unbearable tension and ultimately his heart attack. But Anupama was unable to cry. There was no point in returning to her old house now that her father was gone. Anupama sent some money, which she had saved with great difficulty, for her father's last rites.

Unexpectedly, she got a four-page letter from Sabakka.

In life, one should not take the things people say so seriously. I might have been harsh to you, but that was only because of the tensions at home. When you got married into a good family, we thought you would settle

Sudha Murty

*down well. But when things went wrong, we faced a lot of problems. Please forget all those things. Bombay is a big city and you must feel lonely. If you want, I will send Nanda to keep you company. I am going back to my mother's place. My brother will help me find suitable alliances for my daughters. Your sisters do not have a father now and you, being the eldest, should step into his shoes and look after them. Your financial help is very essential for your sisters' weddings. . .*and so it continued.

Anupama was disgusted. The same person who had spoken of Anupama as a 'bad omen'and a 'rejected wife' among other things, knowing very well how those comments would hurt her, was asking her for help today. All her life, Sabakka had taunted Anupama and made her cry. But now that she was earning, she had suddenly become important. Anupama felt sick. But somewhere, deep inside, she felt she had a duty towards her stepsisters. She decided to send money just as she had when her father had been alive, but have nothing to do with Sabakka and her daughters. Emotionally, they meant nothing to her.

As for Anand, he, too, had shown with his actions that an emotional bond could be broken all too easily. *I am truly alone.*

'Anupama, what are you thinking?' Vasant's voice broke into Anupama's reverie.

'How do you define beauty?' she asked.

Vasant was startled by her abrupt question. 'I am not a philosopher or an artist, so my opinion on the subject is immaterial.'

'Still, I want your opinion,' Anupama insisted.

'Nature has taught me all that I know about beauty. Look at these flowers, Anupama, they come in so many different colours and fragrances; the sky with its myriad shades of blue; and the birds each one so different from the other. No artist can recreate the vibrant colours of nature on canvas. We think we know all about beauty, but what we understand is that external beauty is short-lived. Even the most beautiful people change as they grow older. But the beauty of Nature is permanent.

'Once I was travelling with my friends through the Valley of Flowers in the Himalayas. The sheer beauty of the valley made me realize how foolish human beings are to seek artificial beauty with cosmetics.

'One's beauty is seen in one's nature. A good human being who is compassionate to others, who tries to understand the other person's difficulties and reach out to them in their hour of need has real beauty. Such people should always be cherished and honoured.' His passionate speech surprised even Vasant. He saw a flicker in Anupama's eyes, but did not know that she was thinking about Anand. Anand had been bright, sharp, and intelligent, but very immature! He had never ever thought of beauty in such terms.

Just then, Anupama's students bustled in and, pushing back all thoughts of the past, she stood up to greet them.

'Vasant, this is Vinuta, Shashi, Rekha. . .'

'Ma'am, we know Doctor Vasant. We met him when you were in the hospital.'

Anupama smiled and Vasant felt as if a thousand lights had been lit in the room.

◈

Anand was going to his father-in-law's house for the first time. But instead of feeling happy, he was consumed with shame and guilt. He had known that Shamanna was a teacher who lived in a small village, but he had never thought of visiting him there.

At first he had thought of writing to Shamanna to gauge his reaction, before going to the village to bring back Anupama. But since he did not want to delay matters any further, he decided to go in person to apologize to Anupama. He was well aware that she might not forgive him immediately, but he was determined to persuade her to return home with him.

Lost in thought, he steered his car along the mud track that led to the village. As soon as it came to a halt in front of the school, the village schoolchildren promptly reported his arrival to the headmaster.

The headmaster was perplexed. Even the education inspector always came on a scooter, and that too once a year after giving him prior intimation. Besides, he had visited the school recently, and his inspection was over and done with.

Then who is this new visitor and what is he doing here? wondered the headmaster. He looked curiously at the wealthy-looking, slightly grey-haired man who stood before him.

In a low tone Anand said, 'I want to meet Shamanna Master.' He looked very uncomfortable in the squalid surroundings. All the children were peeping at him through the window.

The headmaster politely dusted a chair with his bare hands and asked him to sit down. He said, 'I joined only recently. There is no Shamanna Master here. He was probably transferred somewhere.'

Just then one of his colleagues who happened to come in said, 'Shamanna Master got transferred to Hunase village long ago.'

Anand was in such a hurry that he even forgot to thank them before he left. It would probably mean another three-hour drive, but he was impatient to meet Anupama that day itself. He wondered what Anupama's reaction would be when she saw him after so many years. Would she be angry or surprised, or maybe even happy? After all, her husband had returned for her.

When he neared the village school, his heart began to thump in anticipation. He was aware that the reality could turn out to be very different from what he had imagined. When he reached his destination he hesitated, wondering what his father-in-law would say. Would he look at him with contempt and call him a coward? He contemplated going back, but only for a moment.

To err is human, to forgive divine, but have I erred beyond the point of forgiveness? I will plead with Anupama to forgive me. After all, we are all human and this is part of life.

He got out of his car and went to the school office. This was a bigger school than the one he had visited earlier. There was no one in the office room other than the clerk who was busy writing something.

Anand asked him politely, 'Could I meet Shamanna Master? Where is his house?'

The clerk looked at him strangely and replied, 'You can't meet him.'

'Please tell him Anand is here. I am sure he will come.'

'How are you related to him?' The clerk's inquisitive eyes bored into him.

'I am his son-in-law.'

'Strange. Don't you know anything about your own family?'

Anand was becoming impatient with the clerk. 'Please tell me where he is. I am in a hurry.'

'He died a few years back.'

Anand was shocked. The news was totally unexpected, but he had come to meet Anupama and that was more important at that time.

Sudha Murty

'What about his family?'

'I don't know anything much about them,' the clerk replied indifferently. 'His wife had come here once to sign some papers and take the arrears of pay. It seems she stays with her brother somewhere near Miraj.'

So Anupama was in Miraj with her stepmother and sisters, Anand thought to himself.

'Do you know where his daughter Anupama is?'

The clerk looked up from his work. He felt he had stumbled on something that promised to add spice to his humdrum life—a husband who didn't even know the whereabouts of his wife! 'So you're here to enquire about your wife?'

'Yes.' The rich and well-known Dr Anand was being humiliated by a petty clerk. But Anand knew that he would not get any information about Anupama from the clerk if he did not keep his temper in check.

'Shamanna Master never mixed with the others, so I really don't know much about him. And he wasn't here long in this school, but I think I can help you. Rao Master was slightly acquainted with him. I can call him, but he might not know the details either.'

Feeling self-important, the clerk went in search of Rao Master. Anand sank into a rickety chair and waited. He was mortified by the fact that he had been forced to find out about his wife from a stranger.

Rao Master came into the office room and looked at him sympathetically, 'Shamanna was a very troubled man. He would never talk about his family, and if we did, his eyes would fill with tears. So we rarely talked about personal things. There was a rumour that his daughter's in-laws sent her back because she got some disease. Some say she's left home and gone to a different place and others believe she committed suicide. Something tragic must have happened to her.'

Heartbroken, Anand left the school in a daze. He did not know where Anupama was, or even whether she was alive or dead. No one seemed to know what had happened to her. But one thing was evident. He had deserted her when she needed him the most and that made him morally responsible for whatever tragedy had befallen her. If only he had not obeyed his mother's wishes blindly, had given his marriage and Anupama a chance instead of brooding over her disease, he might have had a family of his own. But he had thrown it all away in the pursuit of beauty. Guilt engulfed Anand and his eyes brimmed with tears. There was no salvation for the sin he had committed. He would never have peace of mind for as long as he lived.

Anand's repentance was sincere, but it was like the coming of the rains after the grass had dried.

৵

Anupama had left a message for Vasant on the answering machine. 'Vasant, I want to talk to you about something important and personal. Could you come to my house at six this evening?'

Vasant wondered what it could be, but somewhere deep inside he was thrilled. Satya had also heard the message but, rather uncharacteristically, had not joked about it. He looked at life from a different perspective now. He told Vasant, 'I respect Anupama a lot. She is such a balanced person. Even with all the odds stacked against her, she is always optimistic. Life has treated her badly and given her so many shocks, but she is never bitter.'

'That's why I never consider her unfortunate, Satya. She has a soft heart but great strength of mind. Whoever marries her will be really lucky.'

Sudha Murty

Satya smiled and agreed with him.

When Vasant reached Anupama's house, she was waiting for him in the veranda. A cool breeze was blowing in from the sea.

Anupama said, 'Vasant, I have a small wish. And only you can help me fulfil it. I cannot do it alone.'

'What is it?' Vasant was intrigued.

'There is an international medical conference in Bombay. After that, there is a cultural programme. The organizer is Mr Mojwani and I know that he is your patient. The theatre group in my college wants to perform *Swapna Vasavadutta* as part of the programme. Mr Mojwani says that people will not understand the play as it is in Sanskrit. But we will give the commentary in English. Could you request him to at least see our play and then decide whether to include it or not? If he finds that it is not really suitable, he can always reject it. Will you please talk to him on our behalf?'

Vasant was disappointed. He had hoped she wanted to have a more personal conversation with him.

'Who told you Mr Mojwani is my patient?'

'Satya.'

'Anupama, I don't expect anything in return when I treat my patients. Nor do I think that they should feel obliged to me forever. Some people don't wish to have anything to do with the doctor once they're done paying the fees, but Mr Mojwani is different. He firmly believes that I cured him of a chronic infection and is always eager to help me. I'll definitely put in a word to him but the decision will be his. I know only two people who are always trying to help others, and he is one of them.'

'Who is the other person?'

'You, Anupama. The way you looked after Satya, the love you show your students, and your deep commitment as an artiste. . . No one else could be like you.' Vasant's admiration for her grew stronger each day—she had asked him for a favour but on behalf of somebody else. She was truly an extraordinary woman—compassionate, caring and eager to serve anyone in need. She took so much pleasure in everyone else's happiness, and that was indeed a rare quality. Perhaps, there were a few other women like her, but what were his chances of meeting them, wondered Vasant.

He decided, at that moment, to voice something that had been in his heart for a while. 'Anupama, I'd like to ask you something. . .'

'What is that?'

'I came to Bombay to do my Master's and have worked here since then to gain some experience. Now I want to go back to my village and serve the people there. That is my dream. Will you be a part of my life and complete my dream? Will you share my happiness and sorrows in future?'

Anupama stood dumbstruck for a while. She had never expected this from Vasant. And then she laughed ruefully while her eyes brimmed with tears. 'Vasant, what are you saying? What do you know about me? Aren't you aware of my condition? Just a week back, a new patch appeared on my ear. My disease is beyond any cure now. Within a couple of years, my face will also be white. How will you feel then?'

'Anupama, Satya told me about your past. Being a doctor, I know the nature of this disease, and it does not bother me. I admire you more for your inner qualities than your physical beauty.'

'What will your people think of me, or haven't you thought of that?'

'I don't care what others think. I decide what I'm going to do with my life. If you're worried that leukoderma could be hereditary, well then, so are many other problems such

Sudha Murty

as diabetes and hypertension. Take your time and think over what I've said. I am going to be here for two more months. I promise to respect whatever decision you make.' Vasant sneezed and shivered slightly as a cold gust of wind wafted in through the billowing curtains.

Anupama's attention was immediately diverted from the serious conversation they had been having. 'Vasant, why don't you wear a sweater?' she asked.

'I don't have one,' he replied, 'I have no one to knit sweaters for me, and I've never remembered to buy one for myself. So I have reconciled myself to catching a cold every winter.' Vasant smiled and then took leave of her.

୬

Anand was in Bombay to attend an international medical conference at one of the five-star hotels in Nariman Point.

After the day's session was over, he paused in front of the Oberoi Hotel to gaze at the sea. Of late, he had found himself sinking into a state of chronic unhappiness. Feelings of shame and guilt always gnawed at him, and left him feeling helpless. *I did not do the right thing because I was immature*, he sometimes tried to console himself.

As he stood looking at the sea, someone tapped his shoulder from behind.

It was his friend Dr Prakash Apte. Prakash had been with him in England and had now settled down in Bombay where he and his wife, Nirmala, owned a nursing home.

'Hi Anand, I never expected to meet you here! Where are you staying?'

Anand was happy to see Prakash. 'I am staying right here in the Oberoi. How have you been?'

'I will tell you if you come home and join us for dinner.' Anand laughed and agreed.

Anand and Prakash were soon immersed in conversation. The latest innovations in surgery, seminars, their contemporaries—Prakash was voluble about them all, and Anand was unable to cut short the conversation although he wanted to get back to his room and rest.

'Hey Anand, there is a Sanskrit play at the Tata Theatre this evening. Let's go,' insisted Prakash.

The thought of going for a play scared Anand. It had been several years since he had last watched a play. Even when he visited England, he no longer went to any of the Shakespearean plays that he had once loved. Anything connected with theatre had become taboo for him. Plays inevitably brought back the memories of Anupama, his marriage, her disease, the betrayal and their separation.

Unaware of Anand's inner turmoil, Prakash insisted, 'Anand, let's go.'

'You say the play is in Sanskrit. . .'

'But the commentary will be in English. It is being put up by college students and we must encourage them. Even the German delegates are planning to watch the play. We, as Indians, ought to go, too. The Tata Theatre is as good as any in England.'

Anand did not have any option but to go with Prakash.

The auditorium was already packed with people. The murmurs of conversation slowly faded as a voice from behind the curtain started speaking, 'Dear friends, today we are here to enact one of the best plays written by the famous dramatist Bhasa, *Swapna Vasavadutta*.'

The years melted away as Anand remembered another such voice: *Dear friends, today we are here to perform the play,* Mahashweta. *The theme has been taken from the novel* Kadambari, *written by Bana Bhatta.*

Sudha Murty

Anand began feeling restless and disturbed. He wished the voice would stop; but the commentary continued. . .

'Bhasa was one of the renowned poets of his time. He was called the Smile of goddess Saraswathi. It is said that all his plays were thrown into the fire but *Swapna Vasavadutta* was not burnt because it was as pure as gold. . .'

Anand couldn't concentrate on the commentary. Was it really Anupama's voice or was his imagination playing tricks on him?

Prakash said, 'Did you hear that? How beautifully she is explaining everything! I told you. . .'

'Who is the lady giving the commentary?'

'She is a Sanskrit lecturer from a college in Vile Parle. Every year she directs plays and gets the first prize. And the great thing is that only her students act in the plays, not professionals.'

'What is her name?' Anand's voice trembled in anticipation.

'I think she's called Anuradha. My cousin is her student. It seems that young artistes are always looking for a chance to act in her plays. It is as good as getting a break in Bollywood, they say!' laughed Prakash.

The explanation continued in a mellifuous, well-modulated voice. 'The handsome Udayana is the prince of the prosperous Vathsa Desha. He has an exemplary student, Princess Vasavadutta. She is an extremely beautiful, intelligent and good-natured girl. They fall in love and get married. For the good of the kingdom, Udayana is told that he must marry the Magadha princess, Padmavati; but he refuses. But, for the betterment of her husband and his kingdom, Vasavadutta spreads a rumour that she has died in a forest fire. Reluctantly, Udayana agrees to marry

Padmavati. Vasavadutta visits him when he is asleep to console him, and helps him to accept his second marriage. Hence, the play is called *Swapna Vasavadutta*.

'In any community, land or race, a woman always wants her husband to love only her. Vasavadutta was very fortunate to have a husband who was completely devoted to her. In those days, a king could marry any number of women, but Udayana did not wish to do that.

'The exact period when Bhasa wrote his plays is not known, but historians claim that he comes before Kalidasa and after Ashwagosha.'

Prakash said, 'Look at the depth of her knowledge. After watching the play, you will realize what an excellent director she is.'

Anand was not bothered about the play; he only wanted to see its director, and waited impatiently for the play to begin.

Throughout the play Prakash kept up his running commentary, 'Look at the sets, costumes and actresses. Don't they look extraordinary?'

There was thunderous applause once the play ended. The students came on the stage and bowed to the audience. At the very end came the lady who was responsible for the success of the play, and everyone gave her a standing ovation.

In a daze, Anand watched Anupama walk onto the stage as she had many years ago. Then she had been the heroine of *Mahashweta*. This time, she was on stage as a real 'Mahashweta'. Her face shone with the same confidence, the same dignity and the same love for theatre.

&

When Anand came out with his friend, Prakash immediately sensed that Anand was not his usual self. 'Are you not well? Come home and rest.'

'Thanks, Prakash, but I'd rather go back to my room. I have a severe headache.'

'Didn't you like the play? One rarely gets to see Sanskrit drama nowadays. That's why I insisted on bringing you with me. I'm sorry if you didn't enjoy it. But don't you think Anuradha is a great director?'

'Thank you for taking me to the play, Prakash. By the way, the director is not Anuradha. She is Anupama.'

'Oh, I'm not good at remembering names. Besides, Anuradha or Anupama, there isn't much of a difference anyway.'

For Anand it was a world of difference. He declined Prakash's invitation to dinner. His mind was a riot of conflicting emotions. As soon as Prakash left, he hurried backstage. The attendants were closing up after cleaning the stage. It was already late. 'Could you give me the address of Anupama?' Anand asked the supervisor.

'Which Anupama?'

'The lady who directed the play today.'

'They have all left.'

'Could you at least you give me her telephone number?'

The supervisor looked at him suspiciously. 'Who are you? Why do you need her number?'

'I am her relative.'

'If you are her relative, then how come you don't have her address?'

Anand was unable to to come up with a satisfactory answer. But he looked so dejected that the supervisor felt sorry for him. 'Come tomorrow morning at 11.30 and meet the manager and speak to him. Now, if I stay any longer I will miss my last local to Virar.'

Anand came out of the theatre and stood gazing at the sea at Nariman Point. He felt a deep sense of grief and regret. A few hours' delay in getting Anupama's address had upset him so much. What had Anupama gone through when she had been struggling all alone without any money, support, or even a letter from him?

The more he thought about Anupama, the guiltier he felt. He remembered Anupama's words in her introduction to the play. *In any community, land or race, a woman always wants her husband to love only her. . .*

I probably never loved her as Udayana loved Vasavadatta. Though she had all the qualities of Vasavadutta, I did not have any of Udayana's. . .

The next day, Anand went back to the Tata Theatre and got her college address. He called the college, with trepidation, and was told that she was on leave; but he got her home address without much difficulty. Instead of calling her, he hailed a taxi. '46, Pali Hill, Bandra West,' he said.

∽

Anupama woke up later than usual the day after the play. She was looking forward to spending the entire day in search of her next play. The play she had directed had been a resounding success, and she was very happy about it. Satya and Vasant had congratulated her warmly. The media too had sought her out, but she had persuaded her students to speak to the reporters while she herself remained in the background. She told Vasant, 'This is not *my* success. It is the result of my students' hard work, the dramatic prowess of Bhasa, and the appreciation of the audience. I am so grateful to you for introducing me to Mr Mojwani, Vasant.' Her limpid brown eyes were full of sincerity.

Anupama knew that choosing a play for college students would not be an easy task. It would require a sound

Sudha Murty

knowledge of the history, the attire and customs of the period in which the play was set. She was immersed in her search when there was a knock on the door.

Sakkubai had taken the day off. Assuming that some of her students had come to see her, Anupama called out, 'Please come in.'

Anand walked in.

Anupama was sitting on the floor holding some books in her hand. When she saw her visitor, her smile faded and she got up hurriedly. The shock of seeing Anand after so many years left her speechless. She forgot the basic rules of etiquette and did not even welcome her guest.

'Please sit down,' she said, indicating the sofa.

Once, Anupama had waited eagerly for even a brief reply to her letters and cried, day and night, for a single word of consolation from him. 'Anand, please come and take me away from this hell. . .' had been her constant prayer. But no one had come to her rescue. Now that he was sitting in front of her, she did not know what to say. She found that she had no expectations from him.

Anupama smiled sadly. There were so many things that she had once wanted to tell Anand. She had devoted her mind, body and soul to him, loved him without reservation, and in return he had hurt her deeply.

Every second dragged heavily and old wounds became raw again. Anupama remembered Radhakka and Girija's indifference to her; the helplessness she had felt as an abandoned wife who had been sent back to her father's house. She remembered, in minute detail, the moments when she had contemplated suicide. It was as if all those things had happened just yesterday.

Anupama's silence made Anand deeply uncomfortable. White patches had appeared on her beautiful arms, which had once been adorned by green and red bangles. Her eyes sparkled with confidence; there was not a trace of self-pity in her demeanour. Anupama seemed to have grown in stature.

Anand spoke first, breaking the awkward silence, 'How are you, Anu?'

Anupama turned to Anand. He was still handsome but she thought he looked somewhat jaded. There was a distance between them now, and he seemed a stranger to her.

Since he did not receive a response from her, he tried again, 'Anupama, I saw your play yesterday. It was fantastic.'

Hadn't he said similar words to her, which had charmed her and won her innocent heart, several years ago?

'Thank you, doctor.'

Anand was disheartened by her response, but he made yet another effort to draw her out. 'It was very hard to trace your address. No one was able to help me. . .I tried my level best. . .'

'When did you come back from England?' she cut in.

'Two years back. Anupama, please forgive me. Everyone makes mistakes.' Anand stood up.

'Please sit down. Which mistake are you seeking forgiveness for? Please remember that saying the right thing at the right time is what makes a conversation meaningful. Language is a tool we use to express ourselves. It is what differentiates us from animals. Did you speak when you first got to know about my condition? Was it my fault that I got this white patch? Is it my fault that I am a poor man's daughter? Now that you are here, answer me.'

Anand did not know what to say.

'You knew that I did not have this disease before our marriage. You could have told your mother. . .but you didn't. You were scared that I would be disfigured because of this disease. Your mother and sister disliked me because I was from a poor family. They wanted an excuse to get rid of me and your silence provided them with the perfect cover. I ended up a victim because you chose to dishonour the vows you took.'

'Anupama, I cannot answer any of your questions. I can only beg your pardon.'

'Why? Even household pets are treated with love and cared for when they are unwell. I was your wife, lonely, scared and totally dependent on you. All I wanted was to hear a few kind words from you. They would have been my strength, but you never bothered to console me even once.'

Anand found the courage to say, 'Anupama, avva is old-fashioned. She was worried that if we had daughters their future would be difficult.'

'Being a doctor, how can you even say that, let alone use it as an excuse? Nobody in my family had this disease. Then why did I get it?'

Anand was quiet.

'You were worried about your unborn daughters' future,' Anupama continued. I am also somebody's daughter; did you worry about my future? You never treated me as a human being. I was only a beautiful object that you wished to possess and flaunt. Had I known your attitude towards life, I would have told you to marry somebody else. Suppose you had got leukoderma, do you think I would have left you for some other man? A marriage is a lifelong commitment; *for better or for worse, till death do us part*. Wasn't that what you'd said to me before you left for England? Even though you are a doctor, you only know how to treat a disease, not tend to a patient's emotional needs.'

Her words weighed Anand down.

'Do you know why your mother sent me back? Because she knew that you would never question her about it. I was an unwanted toy she had brought home because her son had set his heart on it. Once it was damaged, she threw it away knowing that her son would not want it any more. I want to ask you a simple question. What guarantee is there that tomorrow your children will not get this disease?'

'I have not married again, Anupama.'

'But I heard that you had consented. . .'

'Avva tried her best to get me married again, but I refused. Everything you said is true. I'm begging you to forget the past. If you do not want to stay with avva, we will go back to England where nobody will bother us. Let us face life together.'

'How can you possibly expect a burnt seed to grow into a tree? Husband, children, affection, love. . .they are all irrelevant to me now. It is too late for us. I am no longer the naive Anupama whose world revolved around you. I know what my goals are and where I am heading, and I don't need anyone's help to reach my destination. God has been very kind to me. I have been fortunate enough to live in a place like Bombay where even this mad rush has a humane side to it. I have excellent friends who trust me and will not hesitate to help me if I am in trouble. All my students are as dear to me as my own children would have been. Their unconditional love has never made me think of myself as blemished. I cannot help feeling sad for those women who are still at the mercy of their husbands and in-laws, and are emotionally and economically dependent on them. What will their fate be if they are unfortunate enough to get this kind of a disease? I am not dependent on anyone for emotional or finanacial support and that has given me enormous strength. I thank God for having been so fortunate.'

Anand heard her out quietly, still hopeful that she would go back with him.

Anupama realized the time had come to make her decision clear to him. 'It would be better for us to part now and never communicate with each other again. We met accidentally, but we were not made for each other. Let us part with a good grace.'

Anand understood then that this would be his last meeting with Anupama. He gave it one desperate try. 'Anupama, think one more time about what I've said. Please come back with me.'

Anupama picked up her books, 'You are a well-educated man from a good family. But there is one thing you have not learnt.' She looked at him steadily.

'What is that?'

'You should never call a woman whom you do not know by her given name.'

Anand watched Anupama walk away.

Vasant was supposed to leave for his village in three weeks' time, so he went to Anupama's house to find out whether she had decided to accept his proposal. He was usually a calm and collected person, but that morning, his anxiety got the better of him. When he looked at Anupama, he was unable to fathom what was going on in her mind. The same smile, the same simple cotton sari, the same clear brown eyes. . .

'Would you like some tea, Vasant?'

'No Anupama, I want to hear your decision.'

'I am sorry, Vasant, but please forget your idea. I don't want to get entangled again in the same circle of husband and family. My past has taught me a very valuable lesson. I don't want a family of my own. Please go back to your village and carry on with your work there. That is your aim in life. My life must follow a different path. I know only too well the prejudices that people like me will have to face in a small village. Bombay has become very dear to my heart; nobody reminds me that I am a leukoderma patient. I don't have any complaints about my life here. This is my world and I am very happy in it.'

'Anupama, you won't be young forever. Who will look after you in your old age?'

'Do you really think we should marry and have children so that we have someone to look after us in our old age? That is not right. Others have their own lives to lead, too.'

'Anu, is there nothing I can say to persuade you to change your decision?'

'Vasant, I will never forget your friendship or your affection. That you would want to marry me after knowing about my disease and background shows your kind-heartedness. But I don't want that sort of a life. You should marry someone like you, with a simple and compassionate heart, preferably a doctor, who can also help you in your work. Please remember that whenever you come to Bombay, this Mahashweta will always welcome you as a friend and her house will be open to you. We have become good friends. Let us remain so, and not complicate our relationship by getting married.'

Tears welled up in Anupama's eyes. She went inside and fetched a small packet which she gave to Vasant.

'What is this?' he asked.

Sudha Murty

'It is a sweater that I have knitted for you. Please wear it during the cold weather. Don't worry about me. Satya will be here and he will take care of me. I wish you all the best in your work.'

Anupama smiled and Vasant tried hard to hide his unhappiness. *Oh God! If only I had known her before her husband ruined her life, I would not have lost this priceless jewel!*

They were interrupted by a knock on the door. Anupama's student Vinuta stood at the threshold. She said, 'Can I come in, Ma'am?'

'Of course, Vinita.'

'Ma'am, we have chosen a play for our college day.'

'Which one?'

'Ma'am, it seems you were the heroine of that play in your college days and everyone would love to see you in that role once again. Do you remember?'

'How can I forget *Mahashweta*?'

Anupama started reciting the lines which had been engraved in her mind. . .

'Like Rohini to Chandra, like Lakshmi to Narayana, am I to him. Just as the creeper depends on a tree, I depend on him. I cannot live without him, and for his sake, I am ready to renounce everything. Let society say anything it wishes. I do not care. . .'

This time Vinuta would play the lead role, and she would be directed by the real Mahashweta. Vasant, like Pundarika, would be separated from Mahashweta. . .but in this case, it would be forever.

As they say, life imitates art.

Anupama smiled. Only Vasant could understand the meaning of that smile.

As a trustee of the Infosys Foundation I receive many letters seeking financial help. The most difficult part is to distinguish between genuine pleas and dubious ones.

One morning, as I was going through the letters, my secretary told me, 'Ma'am, there is a wedding invitation card with a personal note attached to it. Will you be attending?'

At first I thought it was an invitation from one of my students, but when I read the card, I was unable to remember either of the persons getting married. The note attached to the card said, *Madam, if you do not attend our marriage, we will consider it unfortunate.*

I had not been able to place either the girl or boy by the date of the wedding, but decided to attend out of curiosity. As I made my way to the other end of the city through heavy rains, I felt, 'Is it worth attending some unknown person's wedding?'

It was a typical middle-class wedding with a stage decorated liberally with flowers. Film music, which nobody was listening to, was blaring over the speakers, while the children played hide-and-seek in the hall. Women bustled about wearing Bangalore silk saris and Mysore crepes.

I looked at the couple standing on the dais. I was still not able to remember either of them. Standing in the middle of the crowd, without knowing anybody, I did not know what to do.

Just then, an elderly person approached me and asked me politely, 'Do you want to meet the couple and greet them?'

I followed him to the dais, introduced myself and wished the couple a happy married life. They seemed very happy. The groom asked the elderly man to look after me. The man took me to the dining hall and brought me something to eat. Enough is enough, I thought to myself. I can't eat without knowing who these people are.

As though he sensed my doubts, the elderly gentleman smiled and said, 'Madam, I am the groom's father. My son fell in love with Malati, the bride, and we arranged the wedding., Malati contracted leukoderma after the engagement, and as a result my son backed out of the marriage. We were all very sad. I asked him what he would have done if Malati had got leukoderma after they got married, but he would not listen. Her family was worried about her future. There was so much unpleasantness in the family. To escape from the tension at home, my son began to visit the library often. After about a month, he told me that he was ready to marry Malati. We were all pleasantly surprised and were truly happy.' I still did not have an answer to my question. How on earth was I involved in this? Soon, the groom's father provided the answer.

'Madam, later we came to know that he read your novel, *Mahashweta*,' he said. 'The plight of your heroine touched him deeply. He took a month and decided he did not want to be like the man in your novel who shed his responsibilities only to regret it later. Your novel changed his thinking.'

I finally put the pieces together.

The groom's father, then, brought a packet to me and insisted that I accept the gift. When I hesitated, he pressed it into my hands and said, 'Malati has purchased this sari for you. She will be very happy if you accept it.'

The rain grew heavier and water splashed into the hall. Raindrops were falling on my face, and my silk sari was getting wet. But nothing mattered. I was delighted that Malati and her husband had made me part of their celebrations. Never in my wildest dreams had I thought that an ordinary person like me would change somebody's life.

Whenever I wear that sari, I remember Malati's shining face as it was that day and the cover of *Mahashweta*. This is the most precious sari I own.

Sudha Murty